Janey's Girl

Janey's Girl

by Gayle Friesen

Kids Can Press

Kids Can Press acknowledges the financial support of the Ontario Arts
Council, the Canada Council for the Arts and the Government of Canada,
through the BPIDP, for our publishing activity.

Published in Canada by
Kids Can Press Ltd.
29 Birch Avenue
Toronto, ON M4V 1E2

Published in the U.S. by
Kids Can Press Ltd.
4500 Witmer Estates
Niagara Falls, NY 14305-1386

Edited by Charis Wahl
Interior designed by Nargis Bhanji
Printed and bound in Canada

CM   98 09 8 7 6 5 4 3
CM PA   98 0 9 8 7 6 5 4

Canadian Cataloguing in Publication Data

Friesen, Gayle
    Janey's girl

ISBN 1-55074-461-5 (bound)   ISBN 1-55074-463-1 (pbk.)

I. Title

PS8561.R4956J36 1998   jC 813'.54   C98-930342-X
PZ7.F74Ja 1998

Kids Can Press is a Nelvana company

To Brian — for saying when, not if

ACKNOWLEDGMENTS

I would like to thank Charis Wahl for her sensitive editing; Alison, Christy and Annette for their insight, humor, and precision; my family for their support; and my kids — Bradey and Alex — for making my heart smile.

1

"This is a bad idea," Mom says, pulling the car onto the shoulder of the highway. A big semitrailer roars past, sending a rock cracking against the windshield. "What was I thinking?" she mutters.

I look over at her profile. She has less makeup on than usual, her weekend face instead of her work face. Her dark brown hair is pulled back into a neat ponytail with just the right number of wisps softening the angle of her determined chin.

"Gran's counting on us," I say.

She doesn't answer.

We left Toronto five days ago and we've been driving across the country ever since, just me and my mom in a compact car. We had blistering heat for the first two days (no air conditioning), blinding dust followed by thunderstorms on the prairies, and torrential rain through the Coquihalla. Greasy fast food throughout.

Still, driving through Ontario and Manitoba was fun. Mom seemed relaxed, relieved even, to be taking a break from selling real estate. In Saskatchewan, she was talking less and rubbing her neck more. By the time we reached Alberta, she was saying things like, "Is it really necessary to have three prairie provinces?" and I knew she was getting tired.

But now, only an hour away from Smallwood, British Columbia, she's having second thoughts? You'd think we were flying over the Bermuda Triangle instead of going to spend August with her mother.

Mom drums her polished nails on the steering wheel, then arches her back in a long stretch. A breeze lifts a stray strand of hair across her face, but she tucks it back firmly behind her ear.

"There's something about this place," she says, her lips pressed into a narrow line.

"What, Mom? What is the big mystery surrounding Smallwood Manor?"

She shrugs her shoulders. "Don't be silly, Claire. I just have so much work to do. The McPherson house isn't sold yet, and you have music exams to study for."

"What was I thinking?" she says again.

"Uh, maybe that you haven't been on a holiday for a gazillion years," I respond. To myself, I add, "That you haven't been back home for sixteen years … even when your father died last September." But I can't say any of these things. There are topics we discuss and topics we avoid. And family is one of the topics we avoid.

My best friend, Julia, has opinions about this. The other day she said, "Your mother is in denial, Claire. Not to mention obsessive-compulsive with some serious anxiety issues." Julia wants to be a psychologist and practices on me constantly.

I can't remember the other ailments my mother supposedly suffers from, according to Dr. Julia. All I know is that my mom suffers. I've known it since I was a little kid.

"Holidays are overrated, Claire," Mom says now.

"You're right, Mom. I think there's an exit coming up. Let's just turn around and go back. I know I'm dying to trek across the prairies again!"

"Smart ass," she mutters, but there's a faint smile at the corner of her mouth, and I feel a small sense of accomplishment.

"It'll be good, Mom. Relaxing even."

She presses her fingers to the side of her head and rubs in slow, small circles.

"Another headache?" I ask. "Maybe we should take a break?" I offer this even though it's the last thing I want. I can't wait to get to Gran's.

"No, no. I want to keep on schedule," she answers.

"This is a holiday, remember?"

"Right." She sounds like she's trying to convince herself, but she's still rubbing her head.

"Maybe I could drive?"

She smiles at this. "Let's see. You're fourteen so, hmm, that would make driving ... what's the word for it? Oh yes. Illegal."

"Almost fifteen," I remind her. At least she's smiling again.

"So you are. And still illegal," she says, turning the key in the ignition. The engine grinds loudly.

"I may only be fourteen, but even I know you don't start a car when it's already running."

She grimaces as she eases the car back onto the road.

"Next stop, a town called Hope and then on to Smallwood," she says with determination.

I take out the crumpled map and stretch it over my knees. Using a felt pen, I trace over the red line of the highway. The long crooked path shows the distance we've traveled to get here. I can't believe we're so close.

"We're almost there," I say quietly.

"Yup," she says, driving well below the speed limit. "We're almost there."

"So, Smallwood's beyond Hope?" I ask, attempting a jab of humor.

"Yup," she says again, not noticing the pun, or if she has, deciding to ignore it.

I watch the brilliant green meadows filled with buttercups and foxgloves, black and white cows dotting the landscape. In the distance, pale mauve mountains frame the valley where my mother was born. This is where it all started for me too.

"What are you thinking about?" Mom asks, looking at me sideways.

"Nothing," I say. I know she won't pursue it. That's one thing about us. We respect each other's privacy.

It's weird to think I was conceived in this valley. Maybe in a meadow filled with buttercups. Maybe in the back of a pick-up truck. Not that I like to dwell on this particular detail too much, seeing as how it involves my mother and someone named Harold. Still, it reminds me that my mother used to be connected to something other than me. Once upon a time, her life was bigger.

A small green road sign indicates the turn-off to Hope. As we drive past, I wonder what a town called Hope would look like.

2

Before we left on our trip, I asked Mom to tell me about where she grew up. She told me the valley had been formed from glacial and alluvial deposits more than ten thousand years ago. It wasn't exactly the kind of info I was looking for.

I open the window now and breathe deeply. "Wow, Mom. You can almost smell the rich scent of glacial and alluvial deposits." I grin wickedly at her.

She mumbles, "Smart ass," and keeps watching the road.

A strong breeze brings a new, ripe smell.

"Whew, what's that?" I croak, reaching for the window button.

"That would be the pig farm next to your grandmother's farm," she answers. "Get used to the smell."

"Ugh. Never." I bury my face in my shirt, using it as a filter.

As we drive past picture-postcard farmyards, I wonder which one belongs to my grandmother.

All I know of this place comes from one worn photo album and sketchy stories. Gran visited us in Toronto once when I was a baby, then again four years ago. I asked lots of questions about my grandfather, but details were sparse. I suspect she was under orders not to discuss him. The only thing I really picked up was that he'd had a very hard life. And that Gran's eyes were sad when she told me.

"Here's the turn-off," Mom says quietly now. She slows the car to a slug's pace as she makes the turn.

We drive into the shadow of a towering mountain that backdrops the cluster of buildings that is Smallwood. As the sun disappears from view, I feel a chill and shudder from something I can't name.

Julia would love that. My best friend wraps herself in mysteries the way a freezing person huddles under blankets. She's always probing me for details about my family.

"Maybe your grandfather was a war criminal? Or a spy?"

"I don't think so," I say.

"A drug runner with Mafia connections?"

"Yeah, right, living in a tight little farm community in British Columbia," I answer.

At first she thought I was holding out on her, but gradually she realized that I really know very little about my own family.

I used to imagine what a reunion would be like between my mother and my grandfather. But last fall, when he died and my mother wouldn't go back for the funeral, even Julia didn't know what to say.

The fields pass slowly, partly because I'm anxious to see Gran again and partly because of Mom's driving. I'm tempted to tell her she could be arrested for loitering, but I resist the urge.

Finally Mom stops the car at the end of a long driveway lined by tall, sweeping poplar trees. "Here we are," she says, looking serious.

I can see a green and white farmhouse with a sprawling front porch ahead.

As we draw closer, I see Gran, waving and grinning. She's wearing a loose sweatshirt and tights, with a lacy white apron wrapped around her middle. She has salt and pepper hair and a glint in her eye that crosses the yard like a lighthouse beacon. She looks exactly the way a grandmother should look and just as I remember her.

I jump out of the car before it has come to a full stop and run toward her. I slow a little as I approach, aware suddenly of the four years that have passed since I last saw her. She grabs me in a strong, warm hug. As I allow myself to be pulled into her arms, I realize with surprise that I am taller than she is now. The top of her head is level with my eyes, and her hair smells like apples and cinnamon.

"My dear sweet Clarissa. It's so good to see you." She pushes me away as suddenly as she took hold. Tears are brimming in her eyes.

"How was your trip? My, you must be exhausted. Are you hungry? You've grown so tall! Did you have any car trouble?"

"Um, the trip was good … I'm not tired but I am sort of hungry, I'm still growing, and no car trouble," I answer, laughing.

Gran gives me another hug. "Dear girl. We'll have scads of time to talk, won't we? Let me take a good look. You're so lovely." She turns me around and I laugh again.

"Mom, Gran's twirling me." I pretend to be dizzy. Then I notice Mom is still standing beside the car.

Suddenly the air feels still, although the trees above continue to sway in the wind.

Gran approaches my mother and the two women embrace, a tentative touch at first and then there is no space between them. I look away because it's too intimate. I think I hear my mother say, "I'm sorry," but Gran hushes her as they rock slowly together.

Sorry for what? I wonder. The front door is open, so I walk inside. The hallway holds the same scent as Gran's hair magnified ten times, and as I move toward the kitchen, I see counters laden with cinnamon buns and pies and freshly baked buns. Something is simmering on the stove. Spices rise up, mixed with the steam, and I give the thick soup a quick stir to keep it from bubbling over.

Sunshine streams through the curtains, particles of light lingering in the delicate lace, and I feel a sense of relief. I had expected a harsh and cold place. A dark house.

I grab a bun off the cooling rack and tear it open. It is still warm. I shove an entire half into my mouth.

"Claire." My mother's disapproval enters the warm room like an autumn breeze. "You might have asked first." She sounds apologetic and tense.

"Not at all, Janey," Gran says with a wave of her hand. "I've baked oodles of things."

"It's Jane," Mom corrects her.

I wonder for the millionth time what my mother is thinking.

"I'm sorry, Gran," I say, still watching my mother. "They smelled so good."

"Well, it's all for you. We need to get some meat on those bones," she clucks.

"She's fine the way she is, Mother," Mom says briskly. "I'm going to bring in the luggage. Claire, will you help?" She asks it as a question, but I hear the order.

As I move past her, my grandmother gives me a squeeze on the shoulder. I feel grateful.

Outside, Mom leans against the car, breathing deeply. I rush over to her. "Are you okay?"

"It was a mistake to come here." Her eyes look frightened.

"How come?" I ask.

She just shakes her head as she opens the trunk of the car and rummages, emerging with her running shoes. "Tell Gran I'm going for a run," she says, slipping off her sandals and lacing up the well-worn sneakers. "I've been sitting for too long. I'll help with the luggage when I get back, okay?"

Her movements are abrupt and tense. I nod as I watch her doing her stretches. Then she's off.

"I won't be long." The wind brings her words back to me.

"Fine. I don't care," I answer. I watch her straight back as she runs toward the gatepost. I grab my suitcase and pull it into the house.

3

Gran shows me to the room where I'll be sleeping.

"I've emptied the wardrobe for you." She opens the doors of the tall pine chest in the corner. The hangers are woven with brightly colored yarn, and the smell of dried flowers sifts into the room.

"It's so pretty," I say. "I've always wanted to sleep in a four-poster bed." I sit down on the white cotton quilt and admire the multicolored crocheted afghan.

"This used to be your mother's room when she was a little girl." Gran's voice is wistful. She straightens fresh flowers in a vase.

It couldn't be more opposite to the brass and glass furniture and polished wood floors of our apartment back home. There, every color blends perfectly — monochromatic, my mother's favorite word — unlike these splashes of bold contrasting tones.

Every once in a while I try to add an area rug or a tablecloth to our place, but the next day I find things back the way they're supposed to be. It's like living in a furniture catalog.

"It doesn't really seem like my mom," I say, looking around at the objects in the room. There are baskets filled with knitting yarn and dried flowers; bookshelves spill over with worn hardcover novels. Figurines and knickknacks are lined up on the dresser, and even the lamp has a fringed shawl draped over it. Mom would have that folded away in a second, I think, recalling her spartan bedroom with its blond oak furniture and cool, crisp lines.

"She used to love this room," Gran says softly, looking out the window. A trellis covered with flowering ivy peeks up past the windowsill. "Did she say when she'd be back?"

I shake my head and begin unpacking. I have so many questions about what my mother was like when she was a little girl, but I'm still stuck on the idea that she was *ever* a little girl. She is the most grown-up grown-up I've ever known. Always on a schedule and so organized.

"Why don't you get settled, dear? When you're done, I'll show you the music room. Your mother says you're quite anxious to keep up with your music."

She leaves the room, softly closing the door behind her.

Anxious to keep up with my music? Hardly. On this subject, my mother was clear: the only way she would agree to spending the month here was if I promised to practice for my fall music exams.

I dump my books on the bed. Chopin, Mozart, Bach. I don't mind playing the piano, and I know how much she wants me to play. Still, I don't love it the way she wants me to love it. And I can't tell her that.

I lean back against the headboard and dig my toes into the soft wave of the afghan. I let the feeling of the room sink into me. After years of wondering, I am finally here ... inside the fortress. Contrary to expectations, there are no gargoyles guarding the door, no stretching rack or leg irons. What had I imagined? The ghost of Grandpa hovering in the corner?

It was less than a year ago that Gran phoned to tell us that Grandpa had died. Mom came into my room to tell me. I hadn't even heard the phone ring, but I knew right away that something was horribly wrong. She wasn't crying, but I noticed her hands — so long and elegant — were twisting and wringing out a tea towel like it was sopping wet. But it was as dry as her eyes.

"A stroke," she said with a hollow voice. "He had a massive stroke. Very sudden. Gran said it was over quickly."

I had hugged her then, and for just a second she clung on to me. But still no tears. After she left, I noticed the towel on the floor. It was so unlike her to leave something lying around. I remember picking it up and tucking it into my top drawer, still creased from her grip.

I pick up a figurine from the dresser, a ceramic shepherdess with a lamb curled around her feet. What had this meant to her? Could every piece of furniture, every scarf and quilt tell a story? Maybe if I listen carefully ...

Reality sets in as my stomach sends out a grumble of complaint. I hop off the bed in search of the goodies I'd seen earlier.

After Gran and I have finished a bowl of soup and too many buns to count, I follow her to the music room.

"I'm stuffed," I say. "I'm going to get as big as a house if I keep eating like this."

Gran looks concerned. "You could use a bit more weight. You and your mother both." She pats her hips. "There's nothing wrong with being a little round, you know. Women were meant to have curves. You're not anorexic, are you? I keep reading about eating disorders in those magazines." She peers at me closely.

I laugh out loud and give her a quick hug. Then I move back, embarrassed. My mom and I aren't exactly touchy types. But there is something about this woman that is huggable.

"I don't think you have to worry about anorexia, Gran. I'm planning on having a piece of that peach pie as soon as I have room. Bulimia, maybe. But not anorexia."

For a second, Gran looks concerned until she catches on that I'm teasing.

"It's good to have some humor in the house again."

I move over to the impressive instrument in the center of the room. It's a grand piano — a Yamaha — a serious music-lover's piano. Photos are spread out over its ebony top. Grandpa and Gran's wedding picture, four or five pictures of my mother — school photos mostly — and my most recent school picture. But it's the black and white portrait of my grandfather that grabs my attention. He has a long black beard and round wire-framed glasses circling dark, stern eyes. It's like he's watching me. The photo doesn't exactly shout out "Grandpa." More like "Grandfather."

"Did he play?" I ask.

Gran shakes her head, and for a moment she looks sad.

I run my fingers lightly over the keys. I play a short prelude and feel the keys respond easily to my touch. Afterward, I spin around on the polished wood of the bench. Gran smiles again and the softness in her eyes warms the room. I wonder why my mother has done her best to keep my grandmother out of my life.

I play a quick staccato piece to keep my feelings in check. There's no point in getting angry. Anger makes you ask questions. Anger sets up expectations and demands to know the truth. And I know from experience that this is impossible.

"My, my," Gran says when I've finished playing. I move quickly into a quieter song.

I don't realize that Mom has returned until I finish playing. She's standing behind me. When her hand touches my shoulder, I tense up.

"That was lovely, Claire. What do you think of the piano?" Her expression reveals nothing.

"It's great." I play a scale up and down the keyboard. "Great key action and beautiful tone."

"I had George Sawatsky tune it last week," Gran says proudly. "He spent two days on it. It hadn't been done for years, but he said it was a fine instrument. I don't think it has been played since —"

"You know," Mom interrupts, "I'm starving." She moves to the door. "There wouldn't be anything around here to eat, would there?"

Gran hurries after her. "Oh, I think I might be able to rustle something up."

It hasn't been played since … when? How was Gran going to finish the sentence? Another mystery.

I push open a window shutter and take a deep breath of the fresh country air. Even on a warm spring day after a big rainstorm, Toronto air has a citified quality to it: car exhaust, oil-soaked pavement, the smell of busy people with busier lives. The air here smells full of promise. Raw and fresh and new, even if it is partly the pig manure. It makes me feel hopeful — as if anything is possible. Suddenly I'm ready for that peach pie.

~ ~ ~

I sleep wonderfully in the four-poster bed, and the next morning I wake to the delicate chirping of birds outside my window. Such a nice change from air brakes and ambulance sirens.

I wander downstairs, but from outside the kitchen door I hear the low rumble of voices. If I move slowly, maybe I can catch some of the conversation.

"... want to leave the past alone, Mother. I needed a break from work and I thought Claire could use a holiday. I'm not here to undo anything, all right?"

I can feel my stomach muscles tense up as I enter the room.

"Is it okay if I go out for a while?" I ask. "I'd like some fresh air."

Gran jumps from the table. "Would you like breakfast first?"

I shake my head. "I'm not hungry. I won't be long."

Mom rises as well, carrying her dishes to the sink. "I'll go with you."

"No, it's okay. You stay here and talk to Gran. I'm sure you have a lot to catch up on," I say, to let her know I've overheard them.

"You don't know your way around," Mom insists.

"I'll be fine."

"Don't be too long then," she adds, turning on the tap and squirting soap into the stream of hot water.

"There's a path behind the barn that leads to a lovely brook, Clarissa. Would you like me to show you?" Gran offers.

"Thanks. I'll find it." I leave the room, taking with me a postcard I'd bought on the trip. Julia made me promise to write her at least once every week.

Outdoors, the warm August air sinks into me and I breathe deeply. Out of the corner of my eye, I see something move. It's a fat tabby cat. Crossing the tall grass toward the animal, I hold my hand out but it runs away. The red barn is easy to spot beyond a small orchard of fruit trees. I walk underneath a large tree, heavy with ripe apples; but more than fruit weighs down the branches. There are birdhouses — a dozen of them, at least — like bobbles on a Christmas tree. Some are tiny single-bird dwellings painted in subdued shades of moss green and taupe. Others are bigger, complete with tables and porches, dressed in vivid turquoise and tangerine, with tiny chimes tinkling in the breeze. I see a tall, slender house painted bright pink, with a small chickadee perched on the top. It's cocking its tiny head down at me. When I finally tear myself away from the little bird village, the sound of chimes follows me.

I find the path and slip inside the shady grove of trees. The sound of gurgling water eventually pulls me to the bank of the stream. I sit down on a large sun-warmed rock and listen to the water music. It makes me a little sad to think I've been so busy with recitals and practices that I've been too busy for brooks.

After a bit, I pull the postcard out of my pocket. It's crunched, so I smooth it out on my lap. I take the lid off the pen with my teeth.

> *Dear Julia:*
>
> *We made it. Such a long drive. I love it here already. Gran's great. You should see the stuff she baked for us … cinnamon buns to die for.*
>
> *It's weird though, being here. It's strange and familiar at the same time. Something about this place whispers my name.*

(I read this line twice, she'll love it.)

> *Have a good summer without me … if you can.*
>
> Love,
> Claire

I lean back against the rock and look up at the sky. I wonder if Mom ever came down here when she was a kid. It's hard to imagine. Did she jump across the rocks or sit beside the stream listening to the water? I can't see it. She isn't the lying-still sort, more of a rushing stream herself.

I grab a handful of dirt and let it sift through my fingers. Grandma and Grandpa started their life together here. Mom was born here. And my father ...

A scream makes me jump. My pen flies off my lap and lands in a small pool of deep water.

"Aha!" a voice behind me bellows. "You thought you could keep this place a secret but I, Sir Lancelot, have discovered you. Where is the treasure? Tell me now or I'll cut you to ... to .... smithereens."

I turn around and almost impale myself on a long sharp stick pointed at my midriff.

Following the stick to the grubby hand wrapped around it, I stare into a fierce-looking face that can't be older than six or seven.

"Don't mock me, you wretched, wretched ... er, wretch. Where is the treasure?" he demands again, his eyes shooting silver-blue rays of light up at me.

"Sir Lancelot! I'd have known you anywhere," I say.

The boy looks delighted. "Who are you?"

"Lady Guinevere, of course. Don't you recognize me?"

"You lie, you wretch. Lady Guinevere has long golden locks. What have you done with her?" he demands, his sword poking me gently in the stomach.

I push the stick away with one hand. "Sir Lancelot, I've had the most terrible time of it. I've been captured by the wicked dragon, um, well, he didn't leave his name, but he was the most horrid, fire-breathing sort and he burned my lovely locks right off!" I pretend to cry as I tug at my short curls with one hand. "And now I'm left with this sorry mop of hair." I think how unhappy Marcus would be to hear his prize haircut so insulted.

The boy lowers his sword slowly. "Ah, of course. That's probably Alonzo the fearsome dragon. I've wanted to capture him for years. But he always escapes. Could you tell me which way he went?" he asks, suddenly all politeness.

"Of course, but only if you grant me one wish," I respond solemnly.

The little boy falls to one knee and looks up, crossing his arm over his heart. "Anything."

"If you retrieve my golden pen from the pond, I will tell you where the dragon went." I point to the still pond formed by rocks and fallen trees.

"Cinchy," the boy says, wading into the water, sneakers and all. After a minute of splashing, he holds up the pen triumphantly.

Then his eyes turn sad. "But this pen is only blue."

I take it from his dripping hands and dry it on my shirttail. "Ah, yes, but it is a magic pen. It only looks blue to the untrained eye. But the words it writes are of pure gold."

A bright grin covers his grimy face and he smacks his forehead. "Of course. Well?"

"Well what?"

"Well, where did Alonzo the Fearsome go?" He looks around.

"Oh, um, over there." I point across the brook to a meadow.

The little boy tucks his sword through the frayed belt loop of his jean shorts. "I'm off then." He starts to cross the stream, hopping from rock to rock. In the middle, he turns to me. "Aren't you going to come?"

I check my watch. I can spend some time looking for a dragon, I figure. Besides, there's something about this boy that I like.

I tuck the postcard and pen into my pocket and follow him, wary of my leather running shoes.

We scramble up on the bank, and the full force of the sun hits me. The little boy steadily wades through the tall grass.

"Wait for me," I call, avoiding the cow pies. The city girl in me has taken over.

The boy stops and waits, his cropped blond hair gleaming in the sunlight. "Which way now?" he demands.

I scratch my dragon-shorn hair and pretend to consider. Then, in the stillness of the warm air, I hear the sound of heavy breathing. The little boy's imagination must be contagious. He is looking beyond me, wild-eyed with terror. He's really good at this, I marvel. I follow his gaze, prepared to match his look of terror with one of my own.

Acting, it turns out, is not required. I find myself staring into the eyes of a very large animal. I am not experienced with farm creatures, but even I know a bull when I see one.

4

My mind races, so does my heart. This is an angry bull, I'm pretty sure of it. His horns are seriously sharp and dangerous-looking. Should we fall to the ground and pretend we're dead? No, that's for bears. I consider shouting "Toro! Toro!" but I drop the idea almost immediately. I'm no bullfighter.

The little boy stands behind me, clutching at my waist. Sir Lancelot has left me in charge. "What should we do?" he whispers in a terrified voice.

"Shh. Steady now," I say to the bull, holding out my hands like that actually might ward him off. He watches us closely. I feel my knees weaken.

He lowers his large head. I think he is going to charge.

Then, from the woods behind the devil bull I hear an angry voice. A man rushes out of the trees, brandishing a large stick. The bull shifts toward him. The man yells out, "Back over the stream! Run. Now!"

I grab the boy and push him in front of me. I don't look back until we are safely on the other side of the brook.

I stand on my toes to peer over the embankment, but I can't see anything beyond the tall grass swishing in the wind. The boy is crying, and I hold him beside me to comfort him.

Then, over the hill, the man's head appears. He crosses the water noisily. The bull stops at the top of the hill, bobbing its head, snorting angrily. Then it turns and stomps away.

The little boy rushes to the man. "Daddy!" he cries.

"Jamie, are you all right?" The man kneels down and pulls the sobbing boy into his arms. "What were you doing in that meadow? I've told you never to go there."

Jamie tries to get the words out. He points to me. "She ... she told me that's where the ... dragon went." And he starts crying again.

The man looks up, a question in his eyes. His voice is gentle. "Dragon?" he asks.

I move forward, embarrassed. I stretch my hand out and he takes it. We shake hands formally, both of us clammy from the chase.

"I'm so sorry. I didn't know about the bull. I'm not from around here. We were playing a game. I'm so sorry."

"I'm Mac." He shakes his head slowly. "It's okay. Jamie should have known." He sits down on a large rock and pulls the boy onto his lap. The child snuggles in. "I've been looking for you for twenty minutes, young man. Didn't you hear me call?"

"I'm sorry, Dad. I was looking for treasure and then I found her."

I sit down across from them. "Are you okay?"

Jamie stands in front of me, his legs firmly planted. "I think that bull cast a spell on me to make me cry," he says, still shaking.

"I bet he did," I say. "I wanted to cry, too, but my tears were afraid to come out!"

Mac sends me an easy smile over his son's head. Jamie looks relieved. Then he sits, suddenly pale.

The smile disappears from Mac's face. "Are you tired, son?" He touches the boy's forehead with the back of his hand.

Jamie pushes his father's hand away. "I'm okay."

"It's time to get you home," says Mac. He takes the little boy's hand. Jamie doesn't resist.

"Can you find your way back?" he asks me. "We should be going."

"I'll be fine," I reassure him.

He starts to leave but, after a few steps, turns around. "Where are you staying?"

"Not far from here. I'll be fine," I repeat.

He nods, but makes no move to leave. His eyes are such a deep blue, and it seems like they're looking straight through me. Suddenly I feel like a trespasser.

"I'm from Toronto," I say, quite loudly.

My voice breaks the spell.

"So, you're just here for a while then?"

I nod.

"Daddy ..."

Mac and I look down at Jamie.

"I don't feel so good," the little boy moans softly.

"Listen, I have to go," he says. "I'll, um, see you again."

"Sure thing," I say. As I watch them disappear into the trees, I wonder if I will see them again. Mom always says everybody knows everybody in Smallwood, so ... does that mean he knows my mother? Maybe they went to school together or something? It's weird to think about this whole other life of hers and that this guy might know something I don't.

"Get a grip," I mutter to myself as I make my way back to the path. It's a small town. Things are different here. He was probably just being friendly. I move quickly through the trees, anxious to get away from bulls with long sharp horns.

Gran is in the kitchen when I walk through the back door. She takes in my rumpled appearance with one glance. "Did you go for a run?" she asks.

"Just a short one," I say, still breathing heavily as I pull off my muddy shoes and place them beside the door. I make a quick decision not to say anything about the bull-charging incident. If my mom catches wind of it, I'll be lucky if she lets me outside without an armed guard. She's slightly overprotective. She didn't even let me walk to school alone until I was in grade five. And then I had to carry a whistle.

The kettle calls out shrilly from the stove and Gran pours boiling water into a china teapot. She cuts a slice of homemade bread, slathers it with butter and strawberry jam, and places it in front of me. Then she pours a mug of tea, adding plenty of milk and honey.

"Yum," I say, taking a sip. "Exactly the way I like it."

"Good," she murmurs, sitting across from me cradling her cup. "So what do you think of the farm?"

"It's beautiful, Gran. I like it a lot." I take a huge bite of the bread. "I ran into some people down at the brook. A man named Mac and his little boy, Jamie. Do you know them?"

Gran's eyes shift away from my face. "They're our neighbors."

"The pig farm?" I ask, remembering Mom's comment yesterday.

"That's right. Your mother mentioned Mac?"

I take another gulp of tea and feel it wind its warm path down to my stomach. "Nah, just the smell."

"You say his son was with him? That's good. He must be doing better. He is such a good boy."

"Doing better?" I inch forward in my seat. "What's wrong with him?"

"Leukemia, poor kid. He's been struggling with it for years. He's in remission but they don't know ..."

"Leukemia?" The word sounds horrible. "He's such a sweet little boy." My voice cracks. I bite into the bread, but the sweet jam seems tasteless. I swallow it quickly with a mouthful of tea.

"Mac just worships Jamie. Ever since his wife left, he's been mother and father to him."

"The mother walked out? On a sick kid?" I can't believe my ears. My mother won't even leave me alone when I have the flu. "Why?" I croak.

"Well, I don't know the whole story," Gran says. "I've never met the boy's mother. Mac came back to take over the farm after his parents moved to Florida. By then, Jamie was in remission. As far as I know, the mother has no plans to follow."

Gran clears the table with a clatter. In her haste, a dish slips and shatters on the tile floor. She bends to pick up the pieces.

"Where's the broom?" I ask.

"Over there." She points to the closet.

I take the long-handled broom and dustpan out of the closet and whisk up the mess.

"What's going on?" Mom appears in the doorway, her face creased from a nap.

"I was just trying to do too much at one time," explains Gran. "How's your headache? Are you feeling better?"

"A little," Mom smiles remotely. "So, Claire, did you have a nice walk?"

I flip the garbage can's metal lid up with my foot and slide the broken pieces of the plate in. "Uh-huh. I met some people down at the brook."

"Oh, really? Who?" Mom asks, looking interested.

Before I can answer, Gran steps up to me and puts her hand on my shoulder. "Would you mind dashing to the store for some milk, dear? I've run out."

"Milk? Don't you get it from the cows or something?" I ask. "Isn't that the whole idea behind cows?"

"Claire, don't be smart," Mom warns.

I hold up my hands to show my complete innocence. "I'm not. I'm serious."

Gran laughs. "You're right, Clarissa. But I'm not sure your stomach could handle farm-fresh milk quite yet. City folks, you know."

"Okay," I shrug. "I'll go."

"Well, since you're going, could you get a cola for me? Sometimes the caffeine helps my headache."

"There's a grocery store just up the road a ways. Nettie's Grocery, you can't miss it. You can take the bike, if you want," Gran offers. "It's leaning against the barn."

Mom hands me a ten-dollar bill. "Just hang a right at the driveway."

I find the bike, big and slightly rusted, nestled in overgrown weeds against the barn. It has a rectangular carrier in front. I wonder if it's the bike my mother used when she was a kid.

The bike lurches clumsily at first but after a few turns around the farmyard, we come to an understanding. The wind feels good in my hair as I pick up speed. Wildflowers grow carelessly in the ditch beside the road — buttercups, stalks of purple lupine, yellow daisies. I'll pick some on the way home.

There's no traffic, which suits me fine, as the rickety bike sometimes careens to one side if I'm not holding the handlebars carefully. Eventually I see a cluster of buildings. A small sign on a paint-chipped building reads "N TTIE'S OCERY." Close enough.

A bell tinkles as I enter. The store looks empty but a strong scent of cooked cabbage hits me as the screen door clatters shut.

I find the milk and cola in the refrigerated case and wait at the counter. There's nothing so technologically advanced as a bell to ring for service, so I wait. Finally I venture a tentative "Hello?" If I was criminally inclined, I could have emptied the register and been halfway home by now.

At the back of the room, a door opens. "Yeah, sure. Keep your pants on, there." A woman wearing a printed dress stretched over ample hips walks slowly to the front. She lays both hands on the counter. "Well now, what can I do you for?"

"Just these two," I say politely, thinking it should be fairly obvious.

"Yeah, sure. Do you need anything else?" she asks, putting the groceries in a brown paper sack.

"No thanks."

"We got fresh cabbage rolls today."

"Oh," I say, having never tasted cabbage rolls and not really sure I want to.

"Only three dollars for six."

I look down at the ten dollars in my hand. "Okay, sure."

"I'll be right back," she says, making her way slowly to the back room.

I hear the scuffle of commotion and a man's voice booming, "I'm not finished." I figure she's taken the food right off someone's plate. She returns, still smiling, with a tinfoil package.

"Only five left. Can't leave him alone for a minute. I'll only charge you two fifty."

I hesitate. "Listen, I don't really have to have them."

"Nah, we don't need them." She slips the package in beside the milk, and I hand her the money. "So, where are you from?" she asks.

"Toronto," I say quickly, wondering if I'll get back to Gran's before nightfall at this rate.

Her eyebrows lower as she takes in the information. "Just passing through?" She leans over the counter to look out the door.

"I'm visiting my grandmother, Elsie Harrison."

"Your grandmother?" Her eyes squint up at me like I might be lying. "George, get out here!" she suddenly yells.

A small stringy man comes out of the back room.

"Look it here, George. It's Elsie's granddaughter. Janey's girl, right?"

I nod. This is that "everybody knows everybody" thing that Mom was talking about.

"She's a dead ringer, all right," George states matter-of-factly, as though I'm not standing right there. "So you're Janey's girl?" he mutters, looking over the counter to inspect me from bottom to top.

I don't know how to respond to this, but it doesn't seem to matter to Nettie and George. They just keep on eyeing me like I'm some prize heifer on the auction block.

"Well, well," he says.

"I, uh, should go. Gran's waiting for me."

"Don't be a stranger!" George yells, and I can hear the woman hushing him as the screen door slams shut behind me.

I ride home quickly, not bothering to stop for the wildflowers.

"She's a dead ringer." Like the lyrics of a bad song, I hear them over and over in my head. I don't look one bit like my mother. And as far as I can see, I don't bear a strong resemblance to my grand-mother or to the stern man in the photograph on the piano. It must mean that George and Nettie Whoever-they-are know my father. Or at least they must have known him when he was younger.

Which means something else ... I'm probably the only person in this whole town who doesn't have a clue about my father.

5

"Where's Mom?" I ask, entering the kitchen.

"Upstairs unpacking, dear." Gran looks at me curiously.

I put the milk and cabbage rolls in the fridge, and hold up the bottle of cola. "I'll just go give her this." I'm tempted to ask Gran about my father, but something tells me this might get her into trouble with Mom.

"Okay. Will you let her know that lunch is almost ready?"

I race up the stairs to Mom's room, but I hesitate at the door. I can feel my heart pounding in my throat. Will she brush off the conversation like she has so many times before?

I knock softly on the door. As she calls out, "Come in," my stomach does a flip-flop.

"Here's your headache cure," I say in a rush as I enter the room.

She takes it from me, twisting the cap in a firm grip. "Thanks, Claire. Too bad Gran doesn't keep any rum around here. I could use a stiff drink."

"Want me to sneak out and score some for you?" I joke, watching her face.

It works. Mom smiles and ruffles my hair, not too gently. "Humph," she grumbles. "So, how do you like it here so far?" She takes a swig like it's medicine.

"It's beautiful and ... peaceful. I like it."

"Peaceful? I guess," she says grimly, hanging her monochromatic wardrobe in the closet.

"Maybe you just have to get used to the pace."

"Pace? There's a pace here? I hadn't noticed," she says dryly. "It's hard enough to find a pulse."

This is better. My mom being sharp is a good sign.

"Well, I like it," I say again, ruffling the lace curtains with my hand. The contrast between the soft fabric and my mother's stark expression is suddenly obvious. I take a deep breath, trying to work up the courage to continue.

"So, Mom ..." I begin.

She turns and looks at me, her perfectly shaped eyebrows arched expectantly.

I study my feet and notice that they're curled tightly. "I met some people down at the grocery store just now. Nettie and George."

"The town busybodies."

"Yeah, they seem like they'd know a lot about what's going on. Anyway, they said I was a dead ringer." I watch my mother's face, but she's giving away nothing. "Which, of course, was a weird thing to say, in a way, since they've never seen me before. But when I told them that Gran was, you know, my grandmother, then they figured out that I was your daughter, and that's when they said it …"

"Dead ringer."

"Yeah. But the thing is, I don't look a whole lot like you. I mean, you're dark, I'm blond. You have big brown eyes, mine are blue and sort of small. And I don't look like Gran, or even my grandfather, as far as I can tell, and I was thinking that …" I stop to breathe, since I've forgotten to do that.

"… that maybe you look like your father?" Mom asks.

"Yeah," I say, surprised by her calm voice. This is going better than I expected. "So, do I? Look like him at all?"

"Why the sudden interest, Claire?"

"It's not really sudden. It's just that being here in Smallwood makes me realize that I'm going to be running into people who knew him, and it seems like I should know more about him …" My voice fades away because Mom's brow is furrowing. I think maybe I'm crossing some invisible line again.

"I haven't kept him a secret, Claire. I really haven't."

It takes an effort not to explode at this, but I keep quiet.

"I told you his name is Harold McGregor ... that I became pregnant when I was just eighteen, and that he wanted no part of it. What more is there to say?" Her tone is clipped. There's an "end of subject" sound to it.

"Why did he want no part of it?" I say "it" because it feels less bad than saying "me."

"I never gave you any false hope about your father, Claire. He was only seventeen ... not even finished high school. He just wasn't ready to be a father. So it was the two of us ... you and me. We didn't need anyone else."

We didn't? I remember all the Christmases when we'd buy a chicken for dinner because it "didn't pay" to buy a turkey ... how we'd go to every holiday event in the city because our few friends were caught up in their own family excitement. A few extra family members wouldn't have been nice? But this would just derail our conversation, so I take another approach.

"You must have been scared when you found out," I say slowly.

"Terrified. You have no idea," she says, looking out the window. "This place is lost in time, Claire. Let me tell you about Smallwood. Monday to Saturday, you get up to do your chores at six o'clock in the morning. On Sundays you go to church, come home for roast chicken or roast beef, then back to church for evening service. Then, on Monday you wake up at six o'clock and do your chores. You grow up, get married *and then* you have children. In that order. That part is very important. And you wake up on Monday morning at six o'clock and you do your chores. *That's* the way it works in Smallwood." She sits down and rubs her head in the familiar way.

"But what's *he* like?" I ask quietly.

She sighs as though the question has caused her great pain. I don't want to hurt her, but what about me?

"I have no idea what he's like, Claire. He *was* my best friend growing up. He *was* the only person who really understood me. But at the end, I realized I didn't know him at all. And I guess he didn't really know me. At any rate, he didn't want me. Or you."

My breath catches at this, or my heart stops ... or maybe it just feels like it, I don't know. At the same time, I wonder if she knows how cruel this sounds or if she even cares. She's rubbing her head, looking out the window. She's a million miles away.

"Okay," I say quietly, getting up from the bed. "Well, thanks for telling me." My voice sounds shallow and distant. "I'm going to go downstairs and help Gran with lunch. Will you be coming down?" I ask, knowing the answer.

Mom shakes her head. "I'll finish unpacking, then I'm going to catch up on some work."

He didn't want me. The words bounce around the walls of my mind. *Or you.*

"Is everything all right?" Gran asks in the kitchen.

She's setting the table for lunch. I open the cutlery drawer and take out the silverware.

"It's the same," I say, plunking down spoons and forks and knives. Blade facing the plate the way Mom's drilled into me. Like maybe the world will collapse if the knife points the wrong way. I turn a knife around to see if it will. Collapse. Nothing happens.

"Clarissa?" Gran says, bending her head to look at my face. "What's wrong?"

"I thought it might be different here," I say.

Gran's hand covers mine. "Give her time. This is difficult for her."

"But why is it so difficult?"

Gran sits down at the table, crossing her hands in front of her. "She didn't expect her father to die. None of us did. He was always the picture of health ... working the land, strong as an ox," she smiles. "Stubborn as a mule."

I sit across from her. "Tell me more."

"Your grandfather had a very hard life," she says carefully. "His mother died when he was six years old, and he was sent away."

"Sent away?" I interrupt. "Like to be with relatives?"

"Not exactly. Back then it was quite usual for a couple to adopt a child if the parents were unable to raise it. Your great-grandfather couldn't manage, what with the farm and the older children, so he gave your grandfather up."

"At six years old? Did he visit him at least?"

Gran shakes her head sadly. "No. Poor people didn't travel far back then. Anyway, I think the people who adopted him wanted him to be theirs alone. Your grandfather didn't talk about them much, but I gathered they weren't very warm people. Very strict, I think."

"Didn't they love him?"

Gran smiles sadly. "Well, now, I think they probably did, in their way. But it wasn't like the love he remembered. The love he'd lost."

"His mother."

"And his father and all his brothers and sisters."

"Oh, Gran," is all I can say.

She draws herself up briskly in her chair. "It was very sad, but he survived and then he met me, didn't he? He married me!"

I laugh a little, wiping stray tears from my eyes. "That's right. So things started looking up for him."

She smiles at me. "He loved it on the farm. The land was a great comfort to him. Especially his vegetable garden. He spent hours there — he raised the finest tomatoes in Smallwood," she says proudly. "For a while we were very happy."

"For a while?"

"We hoped to have children, but it wasn't God's will. Then, after I'd given up hope, I became pregnant with your mother. Abe was thrilled."

"So, that's good?" I urge, hopefully. "He loved her."

"Oh my, yes. Too much, maybe."

"How can you love someone too much?"

Gran looks at me with eyes brimming with tears. "I can't talk about this now, dear."

I feel a pang of disappointment shoot straight through me, but her tired, lined face tells me to be patient.

～ ～ ～

Mom doesn't come down, so Gran and I eat stew and cornbread together. She gives me a rundown of farm life. It sounds exhausting.

"Whew, how do you manage alone?"

"I've leased out the back fields and I'm advertising for some help with the animals. It keeps me busy, all right, but I enjoy that." She gets up to clear the table, but I motion for her to stay seated.

"Let me do it. We want to keep a few dishes in one piece," I tease.

Her eyes sparkle. "You're a cheeky one, aren't you?"

"Yup." Clouds of suds fill the sink and I lower the dishes into the hot water.

"Tell me something, Clarissa, or do you prefer to be called Claire?"

"Clarissa's fine. Nobody ever calls me that, but I like the way it sounds. Mom prefers strong names, like Claire."

"She's always been strong, your mother. Even when she was small." Gran looks thoughtful.

"You're not kidding," I say, looking out over the farmyard, bathed now in a rosy glow from the setting sun.

"Do you love music as much as your mother?" Gran asks.

I'm confused by the question. "Do I love music as much as I love Mom?"

"No, no. I mean, as much as your mother loves music?"

"Well, I enjoy playing but it's not as big a deal as Mom would like." I admit this easily even though I've never said the words out loud before. But then no one's ever asked me before.

"Janey was so taken with music when she was your age. Obsessed, I think — isn't that the word they use nowadays?" she smiles, adding a cup and saucer to the frothy water.

"She listened to music?" I ask.

"No. Played. I never had to remind her to practice the piano. She was quite unnatural that way. So focused. Not now, I take it." Gran picks up a towel and begins drying the dishes.

"My mother played the piano?"

Gran looks like she's deciding something. Then she says, "Like an angel, Clarissa."

6

The next morning I wake to the sun on my face. I don't know where I am until I look around the room, and then I remember. Gran's house. Mom's room.

I take a deep breath of the smells drifting through the door. Bacon and eggs, I'd bet on it. Pulling my ratty housecoat over my T-shirt, I take the stairs two at a time.

"Bacon?" I ask hopefully in the kitchen.

"Nitrates and sodium galore," Mom says without turning.

Gran's flipping pancakes, and I can see eggs sizzling in a pan.

"Galore? You're starting to sound like Gran," I say, nibbling on a piece of crispy bacon.

"It'll happen to you too, just wait and see," Mom says as she places the last of the meat on a paper towel.

"What are you two talking about?" Gran asks.

"It's like you have your own measuring system, Gran, 'Scads, oodles, galore.' But what I want to know is, is a scad bigger or smaller than an oodle, and where exactly does galore fit in?"

Gran doesn't skip a beat. "A scad is only slightly larger than an oodle. Galore, on the other hand, can go on forever. Then, of course, there's a dab, a pinch and a sliver, which are much, much smaller."

Mom laughs out loud. She's watching us with her arms crossed, but the tension isn't there.

"Time and space the Smallwood way," I say.

"Well, it's much more practical than metric or imperial measurements, let me tell you." Gran's eyes are twinkling.

"How about a blob? Where would that fit in?"

Gran pauses for a second. "Well, now, that's just plain silly."

We all laugh at this and, at the same time, I can hear the birds outside the screen door singing in the trees. If I could pull a switch and stop time right now, I would. This is exactly what I imagined when Mom told me we were going to Smallwood. A feeling of lazy satisfaction stretches out inside me.

Between the eggs and bacon, pancakes and toast, breakfast lasts until mid-morning. No one seems in any hurry to go anywhere. Mom hasn't even gone running yet. Another first.

"I thought we'd take a drive into town this morning, if that's all right with you?" Gran looks straight at Mom.

Mom pushes her plate away, dabbing at her mouth with a napkin. "That would be ... fine." There's a slight hesitation. "Or you and Claire could go and I could clean up here."

"I'll help you clean up. That way you can show me all the places you used to go when you were a kid," I suggest.

"Well ..." More hesitation.

"You'll be surprised at all the changes, Jane. There's even a cappuccino bar downtown!"

Mom smiles. "I could use a cup of coffee. I guess the dishes can wait. Okay, let's go."

We take our car because Mom wants to find a car wash, even though Gran grumbles that we could wash it at home. But Mom insists. It doesn't take long to arrive at the town center. Actually, I don't even realize that we are in the town center until Gran says something about the traffic.

"We've even had to add a left-turn signal at Five Corners," she says, shaking her head.

"Rush hour must be a nightmare," Mom says, turning her head to wink at me.

Gran just snorts and tells Mom to turn into a parking spot at the side of the road. There are easily ten or so of the diagonal spaces to choose from. "I need to get some things from the drugstore," she says.

I follow Gran and Mom into the store, but it's so cluttered and full of merchandise that I stop in my tracks. The air conditioning is blasting at us, and the place is freezing cold. "Maybe I'll wait outside," I say.

"We'll just be a minute," Gran promises.

There are some cars driving slowly by, and there are a few people on the sidewalks, but not the throngs I'm used to. I wonder if there's an entire throng in this whole town? Throng. It sounds like a "Gran" word. Maybe Mom was right, Smallwood-speak was starting to infect me.

I check out what Gran referred to as "Five Corners." Shops and business-fronts face a grassy median in the middle of the street. In the center is a tall, iron-encased clock. I lean back against the weather-worn bricks of the building. They're nice and warm from the sun. Across the way is a hat shop (there's a floppy straw hat in the window that would look great on Gran), a grocer and a toy store. Down the way is a chiropractor's office, a doctor's office and a health food store with a tiny cappuccino sign in the window.

I watch the people stroll by. Almost everyone says hello as they pass me. This seems totally weird at first, but then I find myself liking it.

"Hello," I say to an older couple who are slowing down as they approach.

"Beautiful weather," they say in unison, and I nod in agreement.

As they wait for the crossing light (although jaywalking seems to be a completely low-risk option, as far as I can tell), a woman in a business suit carrying a briefcase stands beside them. They miss an entire "walk" command as they stand there chatting. They're obviously in no rush. I can actually feel my breathing slow down as I watch them. In and out. In and out. When was the last time I felt myself breathe?

The clock in the center of the street signals the passing of a minute.

Eventually, they realize they've missed a light, and I watch as they cross at the next one. Then I notice a man and a boy walking out of the doctor's office on the other side of the street. I hold up my hand as a shield against the bright sun. The little boy is tugging at the man's hand, and keeps pulling until he pays attention. A smile crosses the man's face as he bends and says something into the little boy's ear that makes him let out a loud whoop. They cross the street, and as they approach, I recognize them.

"Sir Lancelot!" I say as the boy steps up onto the curb, well ahead of his father.

"Lady Guinevere!" he shouts back, rushing over to me. He flattens himself against the brick wall and looks anxiously both ways. "Have you seen Alonzo?" he whispers.

"Here? In the middle of town? No, I hadn't even looked," I whisper back.

"Oh, he's very surprising," Jamie answers. "You have to watch for him."

Mac catches up to him at this point. "Hello. I thought we might run into each other again. That's the thing about small towns." His eyes are hidden behind sunglasses, but his smile is warm.

"Yeah," I say. "That's the thing."

"How's your visit going?"

Before I can answer, Jamie plants himself directly between us. "You wanna come to the Tasty Scoop with us? I'm going to have a triple scoop, banana fudge, bubble gum cone with sprinkles!"

I wrinkle my nose. "That sounds really really gross."

Jamie's eyes dance. "It is! Last time I lost a tooth! Just a baby one, though," he reassures me.

Mac touches his son's shoulder. "Lady Guinevere probably has somewhere to go."

On cue, the drugstore door opens and Gran appears in the doorway. Her face changes as she sees me. I wave her over. Then Mom appears. It looks like she's talking to Gran, but she stops mid-conversation and her face freezes. Really, literally freezes, like she's seen a ghost. I look around to see if something has happened on the street, an accident maybe.

When I turn back, she's still staring.

"Mac?" she says.

"Janey?" He takes off his sunglasses and moves toward her.

Mom takes a step back, but she doesn't speak. I wait for someone to say something. Maybe Mac is an old school friend? But why isn't she saying hello?

The big clock starts to chime. One, two ... all the way to eleven. Still, no one has said a word.

Suddenly I feel a tremor pass through me, all the way down to my toes, and time stops. Mom's face has lost all color. Mac's profile is between us — it's like looking into a mirror.

"Harold?" I whisper.

Mom puts her hand out and leans against the brick wall. She doesn't look very steady. I'm numb and tingly at the same time, like when the Novocain from the dentist starts to wear off.

"Who's Janey?" Jamie asks loudly, inspecting the forest of adults looming above him.

"Oh Lord," Mom says, still leaning.

Mac snaps out of it first. "Um, Jamie. This is my old friend Janey and her mother, Mrs. Harrison."

Jamie steps up to Gran and peers into her shopping bag. "Whad'ya buy?" he asks, peeking, but not reaching, into the bag.

"Just a few odds and ends." Gran's smile flutters nervously. Her voice sounds strained. She looks over to Mac. "Would it be all right if Jamie and I went to look at the toy store?"

Mac nods and looks grateful.

"Would you like that?" Gran looks down at the small boy.

Jamie nods, but he's quieter now, as if he's finally noticed the tension that's rolling in like a fog.

We watch as Gran takes his hand and she and Jamie cross to the other side of the street. Then there's more silence. Mom opens her mouth to speak but all that comes out is "Oh Lord."

"I think you've covered that already," I say without thinking. Anything to get rid of the awful silence.

The sound of my voice seems to jolt Mom back to the present and she returns to her body. "Harold. I didn't know you'd moved back to Smallwood." She glances across the street toward Gran and Jamie. "Mother didn't mention it."

"Harold?" Mac grimaces. "No one's called me that for a long time." He smiles, but Mom doesn't return the smile.

"No one's called me Janey for years, either."

His smile fades like a tiny bird track in the sand. "You must be Clarissa," he says softly, turning to me. "I knew there was something about you. You — " then he stops short, possibly from my mother's icy stare.

I can't think of one thing to say. All the times I've imagined meeting my father and now I can't get one word out. He must think I'm an idiot. I can feel myself going red in the face, and for a horrible instant, I think my knees might buckle.

"I guess I should go slowly, huh, Janey?"

Janey? What about me! I want to shout out, but I still can't get my voice box to work. It feels like someone's ripped it out of my throat.

"It's Jane now," Mom says in her business voice as she pushes herself away from the wall. She stands firmly in front of Mac, between us. She glances around; people are starting to watch us. "This is a shock for all of us, Mac. Give us some time."

She grabs my elbow and leads me to the car. "Let's get Gran and go." I just nod, abandoning all hope of speaking. I let her guide me across the street because my legs are working no better than my voice box. All I can think of is not to trip and fall flat on my face in front of my father.

7

When Gran gets into the car, she tries to explain. "I was going to tell you. I just wanted to give you a few days of peace and …"

Mom's hands are gripping the steering wheel. Her knuckles are white. "Later," she says.

Later means when I'm not around. The unfairness of acting like this is not part of my life makes me boil, but I'm not ready to speak yet either.

I've finally seen my father. It's too bizarre … running into him on the street like that — almost a letdown. But what had I expected? Fireworks? Harp music filtering down from the heavens? On the street, he had said, "I knew there was something about you. You — " You what? What was he going to say? "You look exactly as I imagined you a thousand times…"? Yesterday Mom had said, "He didn't want me. Or you." I try to pull my thoughts together from the chatter of feelings. He was only steps away … only slightly taller than me. His hair was a shade darker, and thinning. His eyes, so blue when he took off his sunglasses. They were mine, or mine were his. I feel like screaming. Instead I listen to the silence all the way home.

When we walk back into the kitchen, it seems like years ago that we sat at the table, joking and laughing about Gran's measuring system. Mom had been so relaxed.

"Claire, will you give your grandmother and me some time alone?" she says formally, like I really have a say in the matter.

"I want to stay," I say quietly. "He *is* my father."

Mom sighs. "I know, Claire." Her voice is softer, but firm. "We will talk, I promise. But right now ..."

I leave the room before she even finishes the sentence. I know there's no chance of changing her mind.

I go outside and walk aimlessly around the farmyard. At the side of the house, I find the vegetable garden Gran mentioned the other day. The rows are straight and bursting with tomato vines, lettuces, beans, peas and other less familiar vegetables. Grandpa's vegetable garden. The word "Grandpa" doesn't feel right to me.

"Grandfather," I say softly. But that doesn't feel right either. "Gramps," I say. This sounds just right. "Gramps," I say again. That's what I would have called him. "I wish I'd known you."

The breeze picks up and I wrap my arms around myself even though it's not at all cool. What would he say about all this if he were alive? Would he have been waving in the driveway with Gran when we arrived? Or would he have stood there, arms crossed in front of him?

A flutter of lace catches my eye and I look up. A window is open at the side of the house. I remember that the music room faces this way. A hoe is leaning against the house. Maybe it's the one he used? I pick it up and hack away at some weeds that have grown up around the vegetables. It's an unfamiliar motion, and I'm not doing a very good job ... the weeds don't seem to be terribly intimidated by me. Still, it's something to do, and it takes my mind away from the conversation going on inside the house.

"Please, don't give up," I whisper. I'm not sure who I'm whispering to, or even what exactly I mean, but the words run over and over again in my head as I attack the weeds.

When I return to the house, I can hear Mom and Gran still talking in the kitchen, so I go up to my room.

In a way I'm relieved, because I wouldn't have been surprised to see Mom up here packing to go home. The fact that she's still hashing it out with Gran is a good sign, or at least I hope it is. Back home in Toronto, in our other life — that's how it's starting to feel — I always know when it's time to stop arguing with my mother. She gets this set look around her jaw like a dog that's completely unwilling to let go of a bone, and I know it's over.

Like when I wanted to go with Julia on the bus to visit her uncle in Montreal, and Mom's face went into tight-jaw mode in less than seven seconds. Or when I wanted to take an after-school job helping out with the daycare, and Mom said it would interfere with my piano. Five point five seconds that time.

There's a knock at the door and I jump.

Mom's face appears in the doorway. "Can I come in?"

"Sure." This little show of consideration seems stupid, considering how the day has gone, but I say nothing.

Once she's in the room, she seems at a loss for words.

"How did it go?" I ask.

Mom scratches her head and sits at the foot of the bed. Her eyes are heavy. Probably another headache coming on. "I was surprised to see Mac today. Your grandmother should have warned me that he lived here now ... I was a little upset."

"A little upset? Mom, you looked like you were ready to keel over in the middle of the street."

She manages a short smile. "I hope it wasn't that obvious."

"Yeah, Mom ... it was, but so what? I mean, it

was sort of a major thing, don't you think?"

"I suppose."

"You suppose? You haven't seen this guy — my father —" I stumble over the word a bit. "For fourteen years."

"Fifteen," she corrects.

"Fifteen, then. So, yeah, it's a major deal."

"Okay then. It was a big deal. I thought he still lived in Winnipeg with his wife. I wasn't expecting to run into him."

"You knew where he lived? And you never told me?"

Mom crosses her legs and takes a deep breath. "I knew he had married, but that was all ..."

"Did you know he had a son?"

"No," she says distinctly. "I didn't know about that. For a while your grandmother kept me up-to-date on his life, but finally I just didn't want to hear anymore. I know this is hard for you to understand, Claire."

"Maybe if we ever talked about it, I'd understand more."

"I know you think I've kept this information from you intentionally, and I suppose I have." She starts pacing in the small room. "He said he wasn't ready to be a father. What good would it have done to remind you of that? I was just trying to keep you from getting hurt."

"This didn't hurt?"

"I'm sorry, Claire," she says quietly. "I brought you to Smallwood because I wanted you to get to know your grandmother ... but it was a mistake to come back here."

"No, it wasn't. Here feels right, Mom. Getting to know Gran feels right. Finding out about Gramps feels right ..."

"Gramps?" Her eyebrows rise.

"That's just ... it's how I think of him."

Mom's head moves sharply back and forth. "He wasn't the 'Gramps' sort, believe me, Claire. You see? This is what I was afraid of."

I'm confused. "Afraid of?"

"I don't want you trying to turn this family into a, I don't know," she searches for the words, "a sitcom, Claire."

"I'm not," I say emphatically.

"I think you are." She stands beside the window. "Like everything is going to be resolved in thirty minutes. I know this place seems picture-perfect to you, but it's not."

"I don't think it's perfect."

"Don't you? Haven't you already constructed some lovely version of your grandfather as a cuddly, doting 'Gramps'?"

"Not cuddly," I object softly, but I don't think she hears me.

"Well, he wasn't. He was a stern, overbearing man who believed his way was the only way, and if you crossed him —" She stops suddenly. I can see her jaw tense.

"You're not ready for this," she says, and without another look, she leaves the room.

I'm not ready for this? *She's* the one who isn't ready. But I don't try to stop her because, as she leaves, I can see there are tears in her eyes.

8

The first thing that hits me the next morning is that I've finally seen my father. Harold "Mac" McGregor. No chariots, no limousines pulling up to the farm. No horse-drawn carriages filled with white roses. No knight in shining armor. Just the pig farmer down the road, with thinning blond hair and a kind smile.

And it would have been more than enough, if he'd wanted me.

Why didn't he come for me when he was older? A letter, a phone call even? If not for love, curiosity, at least.

I try to imagine having a child out in the world somewhere and never seeing it smile or laugh or hear it ask its first question. I think of Jamie — Mac obviously had no trouble loving him.

It's too much to think about right now. I dress quickly and go downstairs. Gran is already in the kitchen. "Mmm, something smells wonderful," I say.

The table is set with freshly picked wildflowers. Buttermilk biscuits are piled high on a plate in the center of the scarred oak table. Homemade preserves circle the plate in small ceramic pots.

"Your mother said you like a small breakfast, but I'd be happy to cook some eggs if you'd prefer," she says, giving me a peck on the cheek.

I open a still-warm biscuit and spread marmalade thickly on both sides. "No, this is perfect, Gran." I take a bite and the tart fruit flavor bursts in my mouth. "Delicious," I mumble.

Gran looks pleased. "It's nice to have someone to bake for again." She pours tea into two cups and hands one to me.

"Isn't Mom down yet?" I ask. It isn't like her to sleep in.

"She went for a run about an hour ago."

"What did she look like when she left?"

Gran looks unsure and doesn't answer right away.

"Did she look upset?"

"Well now, it's hard to tell with your mother, isn't it?" she shrugs.

I nod. She knows my mother's a mystery, too.

"You look pretty this morning," I say, noticing her gray skirt and white lace blouse. "What's the occasion?"

"Since it's Sunday, I thought I'd go to church. Would you like to come along? You might meet some people your own age."

A thought flashes across my mind: maybe Mac and Jamie will be there.

"I don't know, Gran. Mom and me — we don't go to church much." Only on Christmas Eve, and even then it's a different church every time.

Gran nods but doesn't say anything. Then the door opens and Mom walks in, sweat glistening from her run. She's in blue running shorts and a blue tank top. Monochromatic as ever. Her hair is pulled back in a ponytail. From the look of it, she's been running quite awhile.

"That felt good," she says as she bends over in a stretch.

"Some tea?" Gran offers the pot to her.

Mom glances around the kitchen. "You wouldn't have any coffee, would you?"

The older woman gets up in a rush. "Of course. I'd forgotten you prefer coffee in the morning." She opens a cupboard door and pulls out an ancient-looking coffee pot. "I've gotten out of the habit of making it since … your father …"

I feel sorry for her. She seems so nervous around her own daughter, but then Mom has that effect on people.

"Don't worry about it, Mother." She sounds put out.

"No, no. I'm sure I have some somewhere." Gran produces a container of coffee that looks like it's been around since before the Second World War.

"Here we go."

At home, Mom keeps coffee beans in an airtight nuclear-bomb-proof container in the freezer for maximum freshness.

"It's okay, Mother. I'll just have tea. After I shower," she says.

I call after her. "I think I'm going to go to church with Gran."

Mom doesn't even bother to disguise her reaction. "You're going where?"

Gran steps forward. "I just mentioned it to her, dear. But if you're not comfortable with it ..."

"Well, I wouldn't forbid her from going. *Obviously*. I mean, it's Claire's choice."

I just about laugh out loud. When I was ten, I asked if I could go to Sunday school with Julia. Mom flatly refused. She used words like "indoctrination" and "hypocrisy." I had to look them up in the dictionary. She just likes to think she lets me make choices.

"I'd like to go, Mom," I say. I'm tired of the way she keeps writing all the rules. And I don't like how uncomfortable Gran looks. Besides, the thought of going to church as an act of rebellion strikes me as a bit funny.

"Are you sure this is what you want, Claire?" she asks quietly, looking right into my eyes. I feel like a witness being asked if I want to testify against the Mafia.

I meet her gaze. "Yes, Mother," I answer just as seriously. "I think I'll be okay."

"Heavens, Janey. I'll make absolutely sure Pastor Warkintine doesn't sprinkle her with chicken blood or put her into a trance," Gran mutters.

I laugh. One for Gran. Even she has a boiling point.

Mom has the grace to look embarrassed. "Well, thanks, Mother. I'd appreciate that." She tries to make it a joke, but I think she respects the comeback.

Gran just nods and winks at me as she clears the dishes.

After breakfast, I go upstairs to change from my shorts and sweatshirt into something more churchy. I haven't brought any dress clothes, so I settle on a pair of cream-colored jeans and a cotton, short-sleeved sweater. I brush my hair, looking into the long mirror at the end of the room.

I feel a little nervous thinking that I might run into Mac at church. He seemed like such a nice man down at the brook. Of course that was before he knew I was his daughter. His *daughter*. My stomach does a ferris-wheel plunge at the word. The girl in the mirror stares at me. "Don't be a chicken," she says.

"Are you ready, Claire?" Gran calls up. I try to push away Mom's words, He didn't want me.

Or you.

As I come down the stairs, I cross my fingers. It's something I've done since I was a little kid. I cross my fingers and step on cracks in the sidewalk with only my left foot. It's my good luck charm. Or maybe my prayer.

"Do I look okay?" I ask Gran at the front door.

"Perfect."

I say good-bye to Mom. She seems a little lost. "Are you going to be okay?" I can't help asking.

"Fine." She waves me away. "I've got a ton of reading to catch up on. Have fun," she orders, her voice catching a little.

I hear a blast from Gran's truck in the driveway, and I remind myself that going to church is not the same thing as abandoning my mother. "Okay, see you later."

Gran handles the gravel driveway with the delicacy of an Indy 500 driver. I clutch the door handle and check out the dust clouds we're trailing.

"You like driving, huh, Gran?" I try to keep the nervousness out of my voice.

"Yup. Abe used to tell me to slow down, but eventually he gave up," she says as we take a sharp corner. "You might want to fasten your seat belt."

"I think I'll do that." And do.

We're at the church parking lot in five minutes. A normal driver would have taken ten. I'm starting to feel nervous. I want to ask Gran if she thinks Mac will be there, but I can't bring myself to do it.

I hear organ music. Something by Bach, I think, and we slip quietly into a pew near the back. People are talking in hushed tones, and even their gestures seem subdued, like in the concert hall in Toronto where Mom and I go occasionally. I look around the congregation — Gran says people turn into a congregation just by walking into the building — to see if Mac and Jamie are here, but I can't spot them. That's when I notice that people are staring at me. I shrink down in my seat and nudge my grandmother.

"Am I doing something wrong?" I whisper. Maybe there are rules here I don't know. A certain way to cross legs — left over right — or something like that.

"Of course not. People are just curious, that's all." She looks straight ahead.

It hits me then: these people know of my existence and I know nothing about any of them. Suddenly I'm an animal in the zoo. I move closer to my grandmother and am relieved when a man moves into the pulpit. I try to concentrate on what he's saying.

As we stand to sing, I watch for what to do next. Along with everyone else, I take a heavy green book out of the rack on the pew in front of me and turn to the announced page. So far so good. We start to sing and I'm grateful I can read music.

The tune is simple and the words — although a little strange — are pleasant-sounding. There are lots of old-fashioned words like "cleft" and "thee" that remind me of how my grandmother speaks. My alto voice blends with her clear, slightly shaky soprano. I forget about the curious people around us and lose myself in the music.

After the last song, the pastor gets up to preach. I expect this part to be really dull — Julia hates the sermon at church — but I'm not bored at all. Mostly he's just telling a story. It's about this rich guy who cancels a big debt his slave owes him. The slave acts all thankful and contrite, for about five minutes, until he runs into a slave buddy who owes him a measly bit of money. Instead of forgetting about the buddy's debt, he has the guy thrown into jail until he can pay up. How he was supposed to get the money in prison isn't quite clear, but at this point in the story I'm distracted by a guy who's looking at me from the other side of the church. I look away, since flirting in church is probably a sin. Besides, the guy seems way too sure of himself.

The moral of the story, if that's what it's called in church, is that you should concentrate on forgiving people, not on their guilt. Or something like that. Anyway, I find it pretty interesting.

When everybody stands as the pastor says the final prayer, I am disappointed that the service is over.

Sunlight is filtering through the stained-glass windows in rivers of amber and blue. The hush of the room fills me. It's like sitting beside the brook the other day. Maybe this is why people come to church, to be still. No wonder my mother doesn't like it. She has the stillness quotient of a hummingbird.

Then there is a surge of noise as people mill out into the aisles. I follow Gran through the door, where she stops to shake hands with the pastor.

I look around, still searching for Mac and Jamie, as Gran compliments the minister on his sermon. (He looked much taller — and thinner — in the pulpit.) Then I hear my name.

"… my granddaughter, Clarissa," Gran is saying.

I put out my hand to shake his. "Nice story," I say.

He chuckles and I wonder if I've said the right thing, but his eyes are warm. "So you're Janey's girl," he says. "It's nice to meet you finally. I hope you visit us again." And then we are out in the blinding sunlight, walking toward the parking lot.

Janey's girl. Again. Back home all our friends know it's just Mom and me. But here — here I'm connected to something that everyone knows more about than I do. The peaceful feeling disappears and I just want to leave.

Gran grabs my sleeve, stopping me short. "I have to talk to someone about the potluck next week — be back in a jiffy. Will you be all right?"

I nod, even though I'm not all right, and wonder how long a jiffy is anyway.

"Why don't you go say hello to some of those young people over there?" she urges over her shoulder.

"Sure." I have no intention of doing so. What was I supposed to do, walk up to a bunch of strangers and say, "Hi, I'm Claire. Janey's girl. Elsie Harrison's illegitimate granddaughter!"

Illegitimate. It isn't a word I've ever associated with myself until now, and it feels bad. It feels dirty.

I'm standing beside a weeping willow tree, trying to look inconspicuous when a hand touches me lightly on my shoulder. I spin around like I'm going to do a karate move.

"Whoa!" It's the boy with the probing eyes from church. "Sorry. Didn't mean to scare you."

He's tall, so I have to look up, and wearing faded jeans and a white T-shirt. His face is partially obscured by a baseball cap. He looks like the boys I go to school with, but maybe a little handsomer.

He leans against the tree, arms folded casually across his chest, like he's expecting a photographer to show up.

"My name's Jack," he announces, as though I've asked. "You're Clarissa, right?"

Immediately I'm suspicious. How come he thinks he knows me? "Claire," I respond, hiding behind the stronger version of my name.

"Hmm, Claire," he tries the name out. "Claire. I like that," he smiles down at me, and I draw myself up to my full slightly-taller-than-average height.

"I'm glad you approve," I snap. So much for being inconspicuous.

He colors a little and I'm glad. At least I'm not the only one feeling uncomfortable. Besides, he's probably just curious about me like everyone else. Coming to take a closer look at the monkey in the zoo.

"So I hear you're from Toronto?"

"Who did you hear that from?" I move over to a mound of dirt to make myself his height. But it's no use. He's at least a head taller. And older, from the looks of it.

He shrugs. "I don't know … my mom said something, I guess."

I don't respond. I just want him to go away. A group of kids are openly staring now, and I want to disappear.

But Jack doesn't take the hint. He just keeps on standing there. Then a sly smile creeps onto his face, and I can't help noticing how cute he is. I push the thought aside.

"So I guess it's true what they say about big-city people, huh?"

"What's that?" I ask, in spite of myself.

"How friendly you are." He pulls his cap around

so that his entire face is showing. He looks pleased with himself.

I can't think of a thing to say. I wish Mom was here. She'd know how to handle this.

Fortunately Gran is coming our way and I rush to meet her. But she is smiling over my shoulder and my heart sinks.

"Hello, Jack. You've met my granddaughter?"

"Uh-huh. We were just chatting," he says, the smirk still on his face. I glower at him but Gran doesn't appear to notice.

"Your mother tells me that you're interested in working for me."

"Very interested."

I can tell he's still looking at me, but I keep my stare fixed on the ground, studying the leaves and dirt intensely.

"That's fine. I need help with the animals mostly," Gran was saying. "And some yard work. Can you come by tomorrow?"

"Sure. First thing in the morning."

"See you then."

I can hear him walk away. I look up just in time to see the back of his swagger.

"He's a nice boy," Gran muses as we walk back to the truck.

Not the word I would have chosen.

9

On the way home, Gran talks about the pastor's sermon and Mrs. Wiebe's new pink dress ("Maybe she can't get away with that color anymore"), the upcoming potluck picnic, and how everyone is begging her to bring cinnamon buns ("What are they talking about? They aren't that good"). By the time we turn into the driveway, I have a pretty good handle on the congregation at the Smallwood Community Church.

We park the truck in the garage, and after we climb out of the vehicle, Gran "shhs" me. The transfixed look on her face tells me she's listening to something. Then I hear it, too. It is the distinct sound of piano playing. We stand perfectly still as though we're both afraid that any movement might cause the music to end. Gran looks as if someone has given her a brightly wrapped present.

I listen to the resonating chords and graceful crescendos. Only the occasional wrong note gives away the fact that she hasn't played for years.

"That's Mom?" I squeak. It's not that I doubted my mother played, but this is different. I play the piano; this is like the piano is playing her. And this music is something completely separate from the woman I think I know.

When the playing stops, Gran says to me, "Don't let her know you were listening. Not yet."

Why not? I want to ask, but don't. When we enter the house, we talk in loud voices to let her know we're there.

Mom emerges from the music room looking untidy and confused. She is still in her jogging clothes. She hasn't even showered yet. This is so un-Mom, but I don't say a word.

After lunch, we spend the afternoon playing Scrabble. Mom and Gran seem to be acting as though the day in town never happened, so I go along with it. As we link the wooden tiles around the board, Mom and Gran catch up on town gossip. They call it exchanging information.

"Do you remember Beverly Rabsun?" Gran inquires, putting the word "quince" — whatever that is — on a double word space.

"Of course," says Mom, taking forever to think about her own word. "She stole Marvin Richmond away from me in the seventh grade."

"She just had triplets," says Gran.

"Serves her right," answers Mom, and they both laugh. Mom builds on Gran's "q" with "qat," which she insists is a word. Gran dispatches me for the dictionary, but Mom is right and crows with pleasure as Gran has to forfeit a turn for challenging her.

"I'd forgotten how competitive you were," says Gran. Mom just smiles.

They go back and forth like this into the afternoon. After my fifth three-letter word, I give up and go to the music room.

I close the door and look for Mom's glorious music, but there are only my own books on the polished wooden piano. I lift the bench seat and there it is, neatly piled, pretending it hasn't been played in years. I run my fingers across the curled, yellow corners of pieces I don't recognize, beyond my level. Why would someone with such an obvious gift give it up? The answer comes to me as sure as I'm sitting there. She must have given up her music when she found out she was pregnant with me.

I take down the photo of my mother's father and look at it beside the open window. "He wasn't the Gramps sort," she had said. It was true that this picture wasn't of a warm, cuddly man. Still, the black and white photography gives his eyes a soft, shadowy appearance. Looking into them is like peering into a tunnel. Outside, the tall tomato plants sway in the wind. The longer I look at this photo, the more I can feel his presence in the room.

Mom was wrong. I didn't want a sitcom family
… one with a laugh track and phony one-liners. I
just wanted a family.

～ ～ ～

When I wake the next morning, I've had such a clear
dream about Mac and Jamie I'd swear it was real.

I was on one side of the brook, Jamie on the
other. The devil bull was charging toward Jamie in
slow motion. I tried to get to him but my legs felt
rooted in the ground. Mac's voice was desperate
— "Help him!" he was shouting — but I couldn't
see him. My stupid tree trunk legs wouldn't move.
Then, suddenly my legs were free, but instead of
running across the water toward Jamie, I just kept
looking at my feet. And that's when I woke up.

I'm relieved to leave the dream — I'm tangled
in my sheet and sweating — but even so, it was
good to be so close to Mac and Jamie.

As I get dressed, I wonder why Mac hasn't
showed up. He knows I'm here, so why hasn't he
come? I don't want to believe Mom is right, that
he's not interested, but what else can I think?

When I was in kindergarten, my teacher asked
us to invite our fathers to a special "get to know
each other fund-raiser tea." I asked Mom if she
could find my dad and ask him to come. I thought
she could do it easily — like finding my Kermit

puppet under the bed. But she got angry at the invitation and had come to the tea herself. Charity Ferguson asked where my dad was, and I whispered something about him fighting a forest fire. After that it became easier to pretend he didn't exist, except in my imagination.

When the doorbell rings after breakfast, I rush to answer it, thinking it might be Mac. I fling the door open but no one's there.

"Jack Peterson, reporting for duty," booms a voice farther down the porch, and I do my scared-cat routine, bouncing back into the house.

"Man, you are jumpy, aren't you? You should get that looked into," he smiles, walking past me into the house without an invitation.

I close the door behind him. "Come in, won't you?" I say, hoping he'll catch the sarcasm. But he doesn't appear to notice. "What are you doing here?" I ask, following him as he moves straight to the kitchen.

"I work here, remember?" he says, stuffing a biscuit left over from breakfast into his mouth.

"Actually, I had forgotten," I answer, placing the plate of biscuits into a plastic container, out of reach.

"I'm wounded. Deeply." He plunks himself on a kitchen chair. "I thought you might be looking forward to seeing me." He spreads his long legs out in front of him like a relaxed cowboy.

I'm about to tell him I was looking forward to his arrival as much as I look forward to a summer cold when Gran enters the room.

"Jack! You're here right on time. Good for you." She smiles sweetly at him.

"At least somebody remembered I was coming."

"Well, let me get my boots and I'll show you around the yard. Clarissa, do you want to come along and see the barn?"

"No, that's okay. I promised Mom I'd work on my piano," I say, avoiding Jack's eyes.

"Of course." She walks past me, giving me a quick peck on the cheek. "You're such a good girl."

I think I hear Jack chuckling as they leave the house.

After practicing for an hour, I take a rest. I'm playing better than usual, but not nearly as well as Mom was playing yesterday.

"That was marvelous, Claire." Mom enters the room looking pleased. "I don't think I've ever heard you play like that before."

"Must be the fresh country air," I mutter. "Will you play something for me?" I ask without thinking.

"How …" she begins.

"Gran and I heard you yesterday." Mom's face is shutting down. "You're so good."

She just shakes her head. "I'm rusty. Besides, I need to check my e-mail and see what's happening back home." She pats her laptop computer like it's an obedient pet. "Why don't you go out and get some more of that fresh country air?"

I know I'm being dismissed, but if I could just see her at the piano, maybe something will slip and I'll see who she really is, even for a minute.

Before I came to Smallwood, I thought I knew my mother. I didn't know much about her past, but I didn't think that had anything to do with her and me. But now I feel like I'm being kept out. "Please, Mom," I coax, sounding about ten years old.

Her face hardens and she squeezes her hands together in front of her face like one fist. "I have a lot of work to do, Claire."

Now she's treating me like I'm ten years old. I know her work is only an excuse.

"Not a big deal," I lie. "It was just a ... never mind. I'm going outside."

For a minute she seems curious about what I was going to say, and it gives me a small twinge of satisfaction. Let *her* wonder about what's going on inside my head for a change. But when I look back from the doorway, she's bending toward the screen of her computer.

Outside, I make my way to the birdhouse tree. As I pass underneath, I look up. A few of the birdhouses look like they might blow away in the wind, and the chiming houses tinkle sadly. The gray tabby is looking up as well, patiently hoping for lunch.

"I'd stick to mice if I were you, kitty," I advise, trying to get close enough to scratch his chin. But he darts away and disappears into the nearby brush.

I go for a walk along the road to pick some wildflowers and eventually make my way back to a spot beside the corral at the edge of the woods. I stretch over a flat boulder like a human solar blanket to soak up the sun's heat. I can hear the wind high up in the trees but down here it is still and quiet. I breathe the spicy forest air deeply. It feels like church, only without the questioning looks. I'm glad to be alone ... glad to lie here and stop thinking about everything ... anything ... just for a while. I'm drifting off on a cloud that's passing by when a deep voice burrows its way through the quiet.

"I hope you're wearing sunscreen. The ozone is in bad shape today." It's Jack.

I lean up on one elbow, opening my eyes reluctantly. "Don't you have work to do?" I ask.

"I'm almost finished. Even lowly farmhands get coffee breaks, don't they?"

"Is that what you are?" I ask seriously.

He laughs. "Actually," he says, "I don't think of myself as a farmhand. More like Executive Assistant to the Bovinely Challenged."

"I'll try to remember that," I say. "Did you, uh, want something?"

"Nope," he says, coming closer. He's watching me closely and I start to squirm. So much for my privacy.

"I was thinking maybe we got off on the wrong foot yesterday."

"Yeah?"

"Yeah, but I think I've got it figured. See, you're, what ... about thirteen ... fourteen?"

"Fifteen," I say quite loudly. "Uh, almost."

"Excuse me," he smiles. "Almost fifteen then. Anyway, I figure you're probably just shy around older guys. My kid sister's the same way. You probably realized that I was older, driving ... you know." He stops to point to a truck parked beside the barn. "That's mine," he offers proudly.

I don't say anything.

Jack holds out his hands in front of him, palms toward the sky, then flips them over. "But see? I'm just a guy, a mere mortal. I may look like a Greek god, but I am flesh and blood, just like you are."

I laugh out loud. I've never met anyone so conceited. He seems encouraged by my laughter and keeps talking, walking backward like he's doing some sort of dance.

"So I just wanted to set your mind at ease, let you know that you could come hang with me when I'm working if you feel like it."

I'm still smiling, but not for the reason he thinks. Almost directly behind him is a trough that appears to be almost full of water. And he's backing right toward it. I know I should warn him, but something stops me. Just one more step should do it ...

Splash! And then he's sitting down, in the water. The look on his face is perfect, and I cover my mouth, trying to stifle the laughter. He looks shocked at first, then embarrassed, but I have to hand it to him ... he's still smiling.

"Do you need some help?" I offer. "Mr. Flesh and Blood?"

But he's climbing out, awkwardly. "No thanks, I'm fine. I'm cooled off now. I think I can get back to work." He waves halfheartedly and makes his way, bowlegged, back to the barn.

10

I walk back to the house, still smiling about the look on Jack's face. I wonder if the fact that I'm enjoying the memory so much makes me a bad person.

As I pass underneath the birdhouse tree, I notice a red car going down the driveway. It interests me right away because of two things. One, we haven't had any visitors since coming to Smallwood, and two, this is the first vehicle I've seen around here that isn't a truck.

Then I notice Mom sitting on the porch. Even from a distance, I can tell she's upset. Her shoulders are drooping and she's staring into space.

"Who was that?" I ask when I reach the porch.

"It was Mac," she says. Her voice sounds dead. She looks at me and her eyes are red around the rims, like she's been crying. I sit beside her on the rattan sofa. I'm scared now. My mother isn't a crier. She can plug her thumb with a hammer and she'll yell like crazy, but I've never seen her cry.

"My father was here?" Her red eyes tell me something is wrong, but I can't keep the exhilarating notion from creeping over me: my father has come for me.

"What did he say? What did he want?"

Mom walks toward the field and I follow her.

"Mom, tell me. Tell me what he said."

When we come to the fence, she stops. "I wish things were different, Claire. I really do." She says each word like it's important that I take in every syllable.

"Is he coming back?" I ask, trying to be calm. "Why didn't he wait for me?"

"He's leaving town," she says quietly.

"But why?"

Her eyes are dry, but they're still red and swollen. "He hasn't changed, Claire. Nothing has changed."

"Mom, tell me what happened. I'm almost fifteen, I can take it."

"That's right. Your birthday is coming up, isn't it?" She smiles vacantly, and I wonder where she's gone.

I grab on to her hand like maybe this will keep her with me. She doesn't pull away, but her skin is cold and clammy.

"He said he thought you were beautiful."

I let my brain pause around those words — the first thing I've ever known him to say about me.

But it isn't enough. "And?"

"And there's no happily ever after here, Claire. How many times have I told you that?"

A million, I think, but I don't want to say anything that will stop her now.

"He needed a favor. He hasn't seen me for more than fifteen bloody years and he has the nerve to ask a favor ..." She doesn't look sad anymore. She says the words with ice in her voice.

"What kind of favor?" I ask hesitantly.

She moves along the fence, pulling her hand over the roughly hewn logs. I wish she would scream, yell, cry ... Anything would be better than watching her go numb.

"It doesn't matter. That's not important," she says. She faces me, placing her hand on my shoulders. "Claire, we've done fine on our own, haven't we?" I know she wants something from me, but I'm too fuzzy inside to know exactly what it is. Her words are getting all mixed up with "He thought you were beautiful" and "He's leaving."

"Why would he leave right now?" I ask.

"Forget him, Claire. He's not worth agonizing over." I wonder if she's talking to me or to herself.

"I'm going to my room," I say. I know there are more questions to be asked, but right now I can't get past the fact that he's running away from my mother and me. A slow pain forms around my head.

Up on the porch, I look back at my mother standing alone by the fence. I know if I go back, I'll try to make her feel better, to make up for how bad her life is turning out, again. I open the screen door quietly and go up to my room. I flop down on the bed and look up at the ceiling. When will I ever finish paying back the debt I owe my mother for being born?

In the story in church, the guy who refused to forgive a measly little debt seemed so small and stupid, but now — maybe it wasn't that simple.

Mom had never forgiven Mac, and I was starting to see why. How could he love her and then just not want her anymore? Maybe he *wasn't* worth it. And maybe this was why she didn't let people get close to her.

I try to tell myself it doesn't matter. After all, I hadn't expected to find a father in Smallwood, just a grandmother. That's what I need to concentrate on. Maybe Mom's approach is the right one: fake it if you can't take it.

So, for the next few days I act like nothing's wrong. Gran was grocery shopping when Mac came, and as far as I can tell, Mom hasn't told her about his visit.

Life goes on and I ignore the empty place where the hope had been. I try to fill it with details ... duties.

Gran's impressed. "My goodness, I had no idea that young people still had such a strong work ethic," she says. "This is supposed to be your holiday, Clarissa."

"I like helping you, Gran. Besides, I'm learning a lot about canning and freezing fruit. It'll come in real handy," I smile at her. She smiles back, but there's a question behind her eyes.

When I'm not helping in the kitchen, I practice the piano. But my playing doesn't improve.

"Maybe you need to spend a little more time at it, Claire." Mom says.

"I'm already practicing at least two hours a day, Mom," I mutter.

"How about your scales? Are you spending enough time warming up? How do you expect to get a first in your exams if you don't focus?"

That's when I lose it. I slam the cover down so hard that the keys make a hollow, ghostly sound.

Mom raises an eyebrow, only one. "Claire, be careful."

"I've had it with piano, Mom. I don't care about marks. And there's no point pretending I'm going to be a great pianist because it's not going to happen."

Mom returns to her computer screen. "You're just tired, Claire. Take a break and come back to it tomorrow." Her tone dismisses me.

I would storm out, but why bother? I know she hasn't taken me seriously. Besides, for all her talk about giving me choices, she makes the big decisions for me. Like with ballet a few years ago. The only reason she agreed to my quitting was because the physiotherapist told her how bad it was for my hips. Then finally she realized I wouldn't be a dancer even though the teacher had told her a thousand times in a thousand different ways.

I fume, walking out into the suffocating afternoon heat. I'll just stop playing the piano — ignore the whole topic like everything else and it will just go away.

～ ～ ～

On Saturday morning, Jack drives up in his black Ford pickup truck. The sun ricochets off of its shiny exterior, which makes me think it's just been washed. I'm surprised to see him, since Gran doesn't need him on Saturdays. I've avoided him for most of the week, or maybe it's the other way around. Anyway, I haven't seen him since the day he fell into the water trough. The memory still makes me smile. It was such a perfect moment.

I'm caught beneath the birdhouse tree when he jumps out of the truck and calls my name. It's too late to run.

"Is it safe to proceed?"

I shrug, sit in the hollow of the tree roots, and lean back against the trunk.

He sits on the grass in the sun. He has clean blue jeans on and a black T-shirt. His brown hair, which he normally covers up with a baseball cap, is wavy, and it curls around his neck. His hair looks newly washed, just like his truck.

"What are you doing here on your day off?" I ask.

He picks a blade of grass and examines it closely. "I had to let you know that I survived, you know ... the water trough? And that I forgive you for not warning me."

"Gee, thanks. That's very big of you," I say.

"I thought so." He smiles right at me and I can feel myself go red. "I figured maybe letting someone make a fool of himself was some big-city mating ritual I didn't know about."

"So, by not warning you about the water trough ... I was actually showing interest in you?"

"It's my theory," he answers.

"Has anyone ever told you that you have unnaturally high self-esteem?"

He puffs out his chest. "All the time."

I can't help laughing. I don't believe this guy. Not that I've had whole shiploads of experience with boys. Julia convinced me to go on a double date with her and her boyfriend Rod, but that was a one-time thing. I wasn't very good at giggling, and my "listening to sports trivia" skills were quite poor. Generally speaking, guys make me so nervous that I act like somebody I don't even recognize.

I'm going through all this in my head, so when Jack says what I think he says, I have to ask him to repeat it.

"What did you say?"

He cups his hands around his mouth like a megaphone. "I said, would you like to go to the church potluck deal with me tomorrow?"

"You're asking me out?" I squeak. "The person almost responsible for drowning you in a trough?"

"Yes, I'm willing to overlook one attempted murder. More than one and I get suspicious. So, what do you say?"

I don't say anything.

"The whole youth group will be there, and I could sort of, you know, introduce you to everybody."

The whole youth group? I can just imagine everybody looking at me, watching me, wondering about Janey's girl. What if they asked about Mac? What would I say then?

"I, um, well, you see," I stutter, trying to think of an excuse.

He pokes his head forward like a pigeon. "Well?"

"Gee, thanks, but, uh, the thing is ... I have a boyfriend." The lie is unstoppable, like lava flowing from a volcano.

"Oh. What's his name?" he asks, looking just a little unsure.

A name. I'm actually not a great liar. I scramble about in self-defense. Rod. Julia's boyfriend pops into my head. "Rrr ..." I begin, and then I realize I can't be disloyal to Julia. "Todd," I finish lamely.

"Rtodd." Jack rubs his temple with his index finger thoughtfully. "That is a very interesting name."

I crook my head in what I hope is a cool sort of way. I've seen my mother do it a million times. "His first name is Richard, but everyone calls him Todd." I get up and walk toward the house. Jack follows a couple of paces behind. I turn and continue walking backward, facing him.

"But thanks for asking. It's just that R—, I mean, Todd and I kind of have this understanding. You know what that's like."

Jack nods, and I can't tell if he's skeptical or embarrassed. But then I can't imagine him ever being embarrassed, so I decide he doesn't believe me. I decide to lay it on just a little thicker. It's probably a stupid idea and I'm sure I'll regret it later, but I just want to wipe the irritating look off of his handsome face.

"We started going out last year. He goes to a private school, so we only see each other on weekends but we're, you know, in love."

Occasionally the curse of blushing comes in handy, and now is one of those times. I think this is what finally convinces Jack because his face changes and he looks down at his feet, breaking the stare that was starting to unnerve me, not to mention make me question my decision about concocting a boyfriend.

"Okay, sure. I understand. Sorry about that, I didn't know." He's suddenly so humble that I'm not sure it's the same guy who tried to convince me that he was a "mere mortal."

I'm almost ready to confess when I hear Gran calling for me from the porch.

"I gotta go. I'll see you around?" I smile at him the same way Miss America smiles at the first runner-up.

He grunts and gets into his pickup, and in a whirling cloud of dust he drives off. For the second time in one week a vehicle barrels away from the farmhouse.

I figure I probably won't see him again either. Boy, do I have a way with men.

11

When I walk into the house, Mom and Gran are waiting for me. They're both dressed up — Mom in a cream silk pantsuit, Gran in a print skirt and white blouse with crazy earrings. I'm immediately suspicious.

"What's up?"

"We're going out," Mom announces. "The McPherson house sold! We need to celebrate."

"That's great, Mom. I'll be right back." I take the stairs two at a time, peering over the railing at them. "Where are we going?"

"Into Vancouver," Mom answers.

"That's an hour and a half away!"

"So hurry up then."

I dress quickly in a jean skirt and sweater and pull a brush through my hair. I'm back downstairs in five minutes.

Vancouver. As we cross the bridge to the tall glass skyscrapers beyond, Mom breathes in loudly. "Ah, smog," she says. "It's been too long!"

Gran looks over her shoulder at me, shrugging. "She's always been this way. Drawn to the city." Gran faces the front again. "Do you remember the first time Dad and I brought you here?"

Mom nods. "I was ten, wasn't I?"

Gran cranes her neck to look at me again. "We took her to see *Mary Poppins* and out for dinner. It was fun, wasn't it?" She leans toward Mom. I can tell she hopes my mother shares this good memory with her.

"It was fun, Claire," Mom agrees. "Your grandfather was convinced that most movies were a tool of the devil, so it was an event."

Gran's smile fades, and I wonder why my mother has to ruin the moment.

"Well, it was so different from the way he was raised," Gran says defensively. "You just didn't spend money on frivolous things back then."

"That's an understatement," Mom laughs, but it's a humorless sound.

I feel sorry for Gran.

"Is this the turn-off?" Mom asks.

"I believe so," Gran answers.

We pass the rest of the trip in silence.

"Here we are," Mom announces with a phony brightness as we pull into the restaurant parking lot. But the festive mood doesn't come back.

The restaurant is decorated in shades of rust and forest green. Plants and ivies are strung up in the rafters like the Jungle Ride at Disneyland. Even the staff look like they've been trained by Disney. Some are singing in the corner, others bustle by, smiling like crazy and welcoming us as though they've been waiting forever for us to show up.

Once we've given our dinner orders to an overly friendly waiter named Evan, Mom excuses herself to go to the washroom.

"What was it like between Gramps and Mom?" I ask as soon as she's out of hearing.

"That's a big question." Gran takes a sip of her water. "When your mother was small, she was his shadow."

"Really?"

"She used to help him with the chores — especially feeding and milking. And she'd sit on the tractor with him for hours at a time during harvest. Oh but she'd holler when it was time to come inside," she smiles at the memory. "Sometimes, when he was out in his vegetable garden, I'd find him standing, leaning against his hoe, listening to her play the piano," Gran pauses. "It was really the only time he was still. The music soothed him, I think."

My eyes fill with tears at this. "Then what happened? How did it change?"

Gran's eyes are bright as well. "Your grandfather had been hurt so deeply. He was determined to protect his daughter from the same kind of pain."

"But he was given away ... that wasn't going to happen to Mom."

"No, of course not." Gran hesitates. "Maybe this is too much for you, Clarissa?"

"Please don't stop, Gran," I plead.

She nods. "Your grandfather never got over what had happened to him. He felt that everyone he loved had left him — his mother, when she died, and then his father, who gave him up.

"Even his adopted parents — who couldn't give him the love he needed. Finally, he came to trust rules and order more than people because rules wouldn't betray him."

"But what does that have to do with my mother?"

"Your mother's dreams frightened Abe. They reached out beyond the place where he'd found his security. I think he felt she would be safe if she stayed here and lived by the same rules —"

"But Mom likes rules," I interrupt, thinking about our ultra-organized life.

Gran smiles faintly. "Well, that's true enough. But they aren't the same ones ... or at least they weren't back then. Your mother had to find her own way; she always had such a strong will. Very much like her father that way. They both needed to be in control of their lives."

"What about you? Where did you fit in?"

"I'm a different bird, Clarissa. I thought that loving them would be enough. But maybe I could have done more. Near the end, I felt like a referee. But neither of them ever won."

"Couldn't you stop them? Sort of bang their heads together and say LISTEN!'"

Gran takes a long sip of water. "Maybe. I don't know. I do know that watching your mother leave Smallwood was the hardest thing I've ever done. But it would have killed Janey to stay, and it would have killed Abe to watch her fade away. He loved her spirit even though he tried to control it. It was his spirit as well ... the courage he'd lost."

Mom appears before I can ask anything else. When she sits down, I change the subject. "Glad to be back in a city, Mom?"

"It's wonderful," she sighs, taking a sip of her wine. She looks happy as she leans back in her chair, taking a deep breath of the garlic fumes wafting out of the kitchen.

"I guess Gran's right. You really are a city gal," I smile.

"The energy, all the people ... the glorious traffic sounds — what's not to love?"

"The smog," I suggest.

"The cigarette smoke," Gran chirps in.

"The homeless people in the street," I say.

Mom rolls her eyes. "Poor sports," she pouts, but we all laugh, and then our dinners arrive.

We enjoy the evening, but every now and then I catch Gran looking out the restaurant window, and her eyes are sad and full of remembering.

Driving back through the dusky city streets, a laziness creeps over me. I tuck my sweater into a ball to use as a pillow against the car door. As I'm about to close my eyes, I think I see Mac crossing a pedestrian overpass. I wrench my head around to look, but I can't see anything clearly.

It's time to stop these father fantasies. He has a life with Jamie. And anyway, with Gran, I already have one more person in my life than before. I tell myself it's enough as I drift off to sleep.

❧ ❧ ❧

When I come down for breakfast the next morning, there are clouds in the sky, but the air is hot and muggy.

"Feels like a storm," Gran says, up to her elbows in dough.

"What are you making?" I pour myself a cup of tea.

"Cinnamon buns. The church potluck is today. I hope the rain holds off. Wouldn't you know it, the first cloudy day in a month." She scowls at the clouds outside the window.

"Keep scowling, Gran. Maybe you'll scare them away," I say, taking a sip of tea.

She responds by sending a glob of dough in my direction. It plops right into my cup, and the lukewarm tea splashes up into my face. We start giggling, and by the time Mom walks into the room, we're both wiping away tears of laughter. "What's going on?" she asks.

"Food fight," I manage to get out through laughter too delicious to stop.

Gran has streaks of flour on her face. "She started it," she says. Nothing is really funny anymore; it just feels good to laugh.

"You're both crazy," Mom announces, pouring herself a cup of coffee. But she looks relaxed.

"Would you like to come to the picnic?" Gran asks once she has her laughter under control.

"Sure," I answer immediately and then remember Jack will be there. Oh well, he'll probably stay as far away as he can. "Sounds like a plan, Mom?"

"I don't think so," she answers.

Gran rolls the dough out on the counter and says carefully, "Some of your old friends will probably be there."

"C'mon, Mom. It'll be fun," I urge.

"I have work I should be doing."

"I don't think a holiday is technically a holiday if you work all the time," I say. "Then it's just called … work."

Gran stops rolling and waits.

"I suppose I could go for a while," Mom says slowly, putting a slice of bread in the toaster.

She doesn't sound too excited about the idea, but I decide to ignore it and let out a small cheer.

She grimaces. "It's not unheard of for me to go to a picnic, Claire. I do know how to have fun." She sounds put out.

"Sure you do, Mom," I laugh. "They call her the Queen of Mirth back home, Gran," I say as I leave the room.

I change my clothes three times before deciding to wear what I had on in the first place. I go downstairs to help Gran load the trunk with lawn chairs, blankets, coolers and picnic baskets. "Did you pack enough food for the whole church?" I ask.

"Cheeky," Gran responds.

After we've finished, we wait for my mom in the truck. Gran lays on the horn like an impatient trucker. "I see she still has a problem with punctuality," she mutters.

I kind of enjoy seeing Gran get crabby. It's nice to know she isn't perfect.

When Mom finally emerges from the house, I'm shocked by her appearance. She has on blue jeans and a bright white cotton T-shirt with a red sweater tied around her hips. It's definitely unmonochromatic. Her hair is pulled back in a high ponytail, and she's wearing almost no makeup. She looks about twenty-five years old.

"Stunning," I say, sliding over to make room for her.

"Phhht." She pretends to toss away the compliment, but I know she's pleased.

"We're off," Gran announces, putting the truck in gear and pressing down heavily on the gas pedal. Mom and I hold on for our lives as we turn out of the driveway onto the road.

Gran avoids the bumps and potholes like she was born to it. "I bet Margaret Menzies is going to bring her award-winning apple pie again this year," she says to no one in particular.

Mom laughs and nudges me. "And she says I'm competitive!"

Gran snorts. "No such thing. It's a decent pie — just that first prize that drives me crazy. One country fair — at least ten years ago — but she still manages to get it into every conversation like it happened yesterday."

Mom looks out the window and a wistful expression crosses her face. "A lot of things feel like they happened just yesterday."

When we arrive at the picnic grounds, there is a large crowd, and I can feel Mom tensing up.

"It'll be okay," I whisper as we get out of the truck.

She squeezes my hand when a piercing shriek rings out.

Mom stops and looks around, and then she actually screams, too. I look at Gran as Mom rushes to meet the shrieking woman and they embrace.

"Ruth Jenkins. She and your mother were thick as thieves growing up."

"Janey, you haven't changed a bit!" The woman shrieks again. Maybe this is her natural voice.

"Neither have you," Mom smiles. Lying, I assume, because this Ruth person couldn't have looked this frumpy in high school.

"Is this Clarissa?" she asks.

"Uh-huh," Mom answers, pulling me to her. She doesn't bother to correct the name to Claire.

The woman takes both my hands and inspects me closely. "It's nice to meet you, Clarissa. Your mother and I grew up together."

"It's nice to meet you, too," I say. Her grip is so tight I can't move my fingers. She's looking me up and down, side to side like I'm the mugger in a police lineup. Except she's smiling. "Just so nice to meet you," she repeats. Suddenly she lets go and turns back to Mom. The two start talking at the same time.

Gran whispers to me, "She'll talk your head off, that one. I always had a headache when she'd been over for the day."

Ruth is leading my mother across the grass. "Come meet my brood. They're loud and obnoxious, the lot of them." And they walk off.

"I wonder where they got that from," Gran grins, piling my arms with lawn chairs and blankets.

I smile at Gran's sarcasm. She definitely reminds me of Mom when she does that.

Gran and a lady are deep in conversation when I feel a hand on my shoulder.

"Hi, Jack," I say casually, not even turning around.

"See how connected we are? You didn't even have to look to know who I was," he crows triumphantly.

Right. I spread out the blanket before looking at him. When I do, my heart seems to skip, so I quickly look away.

"Clarissa, dear, will you bring the cinnamon buns?" Gran calls out.

"Oh, Elsie, you didn't bring those marvelous buns again," the lady gushes. "No one will even look at my award-winning apple pie now."

I hurry back to the truck, grateful for the job. But Jack trots behind.

"I wasn't sure you'd come. I thought maybe you and Rtodd had an agreement not to appear at public functions alone."

I let him catch up. "Actually, most of his friends just call him Todd. It's not so formal," I say.

"Okay, then. Todd." He pronounces the word, giving the "T" more attention than necessary. "So, tell me about this guy. What's he like?"

I cringe inside. Details. More lies. But what else can I do? Just blurt out "I made him up"? I don't think so.

"He plays football," I say instead.

"What position?"

"Um, fastback."

Jack looks at me curiously. "A specialty player, huh? Quarterback, halfback … fullback, even, but I've never heard of a fastback. Must be another big-city thing, huh?"

I glare. "Halfback, then, whatever. I'm not a big fan of the game." I try to brush the mistake away like it's a bug.

"But I bet he scores a lot of goals." Jack's smirking again.

"Touchdowns, moron," I say, sticking out a leg. I catch him off guard, and he trips, nearly falling.

"You know," he says, once he's firmly on his feet again. "You have some very violent tendencies. First, the attempted murder at the water trough and now assault. If this was grade four, I'd swear you liked me." His eyes meet mine, and I feel the redness creeping up my neck.

I rush over to hand Gran the buns.

"Thanks, dear. Oh, hello, Jack. It's nice to see you here."

"Hi, Mrs. H. Make sure I get one of those, okay?" He points to the gooey buns she's unwrapping.

"I don't think it will spoil your appetite if you have one right now," she says, tearing off a huge roll and giving it to him on a napkin.

He rips off a piece immediately and scarfs it down. "You're the best, Mrs. H."

I roll my eyes at the obvious sucking-up. What a major flirt. But Gran doesn't seem to mind.

"How's Marcia?" she asks.

"Good. I think she's got a few days left, but I'll check on her later," he answers, polishing off the bun in one messy gulp.

"Who's Marcia?" I ask.

"My one true love," says Jack.

"One of the cows," Gran grins. "She's about to calve. Your grandfather thought it was silly to give them names, but it made sense to me."

"Besides, she looks like a Marcia."

I check to see if Jack is making fun of Gran, but he looks totally serious.

"I'll introduce you sometime," he says to me.

"Sure."

Gran's watching us carefully. "Why don't you introduce my granddaughter to some young humans instead," she orders. "I have to get the food set up." She walks away to join the other women busily setting out baskets and bowls of potato salad, fried chicken, cookies and chocolate cakes.

I shrug. "You don't have to hang around if you don't want to."

He shrugs back. "I don't mind. Unless you don't want me to. You can tell Rtodd that I was just making sure nobody hit on you."

"He'll appreciate it," I answer, enjoying the

prospect of a jealous boyfriend, even if he doesn't really exist.

As we walk over to a group of kids, I get nervous. And as we get closer, I can feel a silence descending.

"Hey, everybody," Jack says confidently. "This is Claire. Claire," he turns to me, "this is everybody."

"Everybody" looks at me.

Then a girl says loudly, "I thought your name was Clarissa." She states it like an accusation.

They've been talking about me. Like last week at church. I am "Janey's girl." Janey's illegitimate girl.

12

A couple of seconds pass before I realize that people are introducing themselves to me. I nod vacantly, pretending I'm taking it all in, but I don't catch any of their names except for the girl who accused me of being Clarissa. Her name is Darlene Jenkins. I realize she must be my mother's friend's daughter — which explains why she seems to think she knows me.

Gradually a conversation takes over that doesn't include me, and I'm relieved. I tap Jack on the shoulder. "I'm going to see if Gran needs some help. See you later." I leave quickly before I can see the reaction on his face. I just want to disappear with a poof. Janey's invisible girl.

I almost make it to the picnic tables when Jack catches up with me.

"Are you all right?" he asks. The kindness in his eyes throws me off.

"Yeah, I'm fine. I'm not big on crowds. You should go back to your friends."

He looks unsure. "If that's what you want." He starts to go but stops after a couple of steps. "Listen, I don't want to be a pest, okay? But if you want to go for a walk to the river or something, we could do that."

I shuffle around, looking down at my feet.

"I know you have a boyfriend, Claire. I'm not really as much of a jerk as I pretend to be. If you want to be friends, that's fine with me. Honestly. I just enjoy bugging you." He looks almost shy.

"You're not a jerk," I say adamantly. If anyone was being a jerk around here, it would have to be me. Jack, at least, wasn't inventing entire human beings. "Yeah, I'd like a walk."

He takes me to a path in the woods, and for the next ten minutes we walk in a comfortable silence. Totally unlike the silence when everyone stared at me as if I was a creature from another dimension.

When we arrive at the riverbank, it feels like something has changed between us. Suddenly I know I have to tell him the truth about Rtodd.

"Jack, there's something I want to tell you."

He looks at me expectantly.

"I, well, you see." I chicken out. "I've never seen a calf being born." I kick myself for being such a coward. Why can't I tell him?

Jack looks at me far too seriously. "Thanks for telling me, Claire. That can't have been easy for you."

I laugh, but inside something melts at the way he says my name.

I can't tell him about Rtodd, not yet. I am not about to make a fool of myself by falling for this guy, and until I get myself under control, I need the lie.

I move over to the river, picking up a flat rock, sending it skipping across the water.

"Not bad," he says, picking up his own rock. "But check out the wrist action." He sends the rock flying, but it's swallowed up by the water in one tiny gulp.

"Very impressive." I send another rock skipping five, six, seven times across.

He slumps down on a boulder, pretending to look discouraged. "So much for being macho."

I sit on a log across from him. The clouds are growing thicker. I pull my sweater tightly around me as a breeze blows up off the water.

"Are you cold? We could go back."

"No, I'm fine."

"You say that a lot. So, why are you and your mother here anyway?" he asks.

"Just visiting."

"But you've never visited before. I'd have noticed."

I look to see if he's flirting again but he looks sincere.

"We've been busy."

Jack doesn't push it.

For a while I listen to the even rush of the flowing water. Questions are pushing through me with the same force of the water moving beside me.

"What do you know about a guy named Mac McGregor?" I ask.

Jack looks up curiously. "Not much. He runs his dad's farm. He moved back here about a year ago so his parents could retire — Florida. I don't see him much. He has a son, Jamie. He's been pretty sick. The boy, I mean."

"He's my father," I say. Hearing the words out loud makes me shiver.

"I know," he says, almost apologetically.

"I guess everybody knows, huh?"

"It's a small town, Claire." He looks like he wants to say more but holds back. "It's not such a big deal."

"It is to me," I say quietly.

"I didn't ... I meant ..." he takes a breath. "I'm sorry."

"You don't have to be sorry. It's all really new to me. I just found out," I explain.

Jack looks shocked. "You never knew? Like, for your whole life?"

I smile weakly. "Yeah, like for my whole life."

"I don't get it," he says, shaking his head.

"My mom, she's kind of private."

"I'll say. But he's your father. Didn't she … Didn't you ever ask about it when you were a little kid?" His voice is incredulous.

"Of course I did," I snap, walking away on the uneven rocks.

Jack follows a few steps behind, and for a time we just walk along the bank of the river.

"I'm always apologizing to you," he says.

"Don't. You see, that's the thing. I never knew it was weird. It just seemed normal, you know?" Jack remains silent and I'm grateful. "I grew up thinking there were things you just weren't supposed to talk about. Like my grandfather. Nobody ever told me about him either. And I hardly ever saw Gran, so it was just my mom and me. Now that seems kind of lonely, but I didn't know any different."

I bend down to the river and feel the force of the current against my fingers. I take a deep breath. "I grew up thinking that it was me, you know? Like maybe I was the secret?"

Jack watches as though he's trying to understand. But I know he can't. How could he? It makes no sense to me either.

"Listen, it's just the way it is. Mac's got Jamie and I guess that's enough. I need to forget about him."

I walk away, not wanting Jack to see me anymore. But I feel his hands on my shoulders. It feels so good to be touched that I let him hug me.

That's the way Mom finds us. I don't hear her approach, but suddenly she is calling my name and I hear the frosty disapproval.

Jack lets go of me instantly. I feel like we've been caught doing something horribly wrong.

"We went for a walk," I manage to stammer out.

"I can see that. Everyone's eating already. Let's go." It is a command.

I apologize to Jack with my eyes, but he seems embarrassed and angry.

"I'll stay here for a while," he says.

"Okay."

Once we are far into the woods, I pull at my mother's arm to slow her strong, angry strides. But when she looks at me, her eyes are furious, and I feel my own anger slink away, outclassed.

"You didn't tell anyone where you'd gone. Didn't you think I'd worry? And then to find you here ... with that boy."

She says "that boy" like the words leave a bad taste in her mouth.

"We were only gone for ..." I check my watch. "Half an hour. We were just talking."

"It didn't look like just talking."

I don't know what to say. If I tell her we were discussing Mac, she'll be even angrier. I can't explain the hug without telling her everything, and I can't tell her everything ... because we don't do that.

"Just forget it," I say quietly. I try to walk past her but she grabs my arm roughly. For a second I think she might actually slap me, and I shrink back against a tree.

She drops my arm as suddenly as she grabbed it. I pull back, rubbing my upper arm where her grip had tightened.

Her eyes widen. "I'm sorry."

We make our way back in silence. But it's different than the quiet I shared with Jack. This time it feels heavy with unspoken words.

It's starting to rain and people are moving the tables under the trees; but Gran just takes one look at Mom, and gets ready to leave. She seems to know not to ask any questions, and we drive back to the farmhouse without a word.

I spend the rest of the afternoon in my room. I decide to write to Julia, so I go into the desk drawer, looking for writing paper. I rummage around, but there's just a bunch of old junk. A couple of miniature rusty license plates that say "Jane" and "Ruth," some broken pencils and chewed-up pen lids. Then, at the back of the drawer, I find a small book. The cover is navy blue with a white label on the front. Inscribed, in messy handwriting, are the words "MY DIARY." The handwriting is rounder than it is now, but I recognize it immediately: it's my mother's.

I sit and look at the book like it's a genie's lamp, wondering what might come out. There's no lock on it. All I have to do is flip open the cover and read my mother's words. I can reach back in time — but something stops me. Opening this book would betray her.

Reluctantly, I return the diary to the drawer and slide it closed.

I know I should go down for supper, if only for Gran. She doesn't deserve to be in the middle of all this. As I walk down the stairs, I wonder what my mother has told her about this afternoon.

They're talking quietly when I enter the kitchen. The air smells of sautéed celery, onions and garlic.

"Smells wonderful," I say, suddenly aware that I haven't eaten since breakfast.

"Let me get you some soup, dear," Gran says.

"I'll get it, Gran."

I take a bowl out of the cupboard and fill it with the thick vegetable broth.

Gran gets up anyway and cuts thick slices of garden tomatoes and cucumbers for me. I smile a thank you.

Then the phone rings and she goes into the living room to take the call, ignoring the phone that's right beside her.

The silence in the kitchen is deafening.

"Good soup, isn't it?" Mom gives in first.

I grunt agreement, slurping loudly.

"It's one of my favorites," she says, then, "Claire, I'm sorry about what happened today. I overreacted."

"I guess," I say, without looking up.

"It's just that I'd never seen that boy before and —"

"His name is Jack," I interrupt.

"Yes. Your grandmother just told me that he works for her."

"He's been here all week. You never noticed?"

"I guess I've been a little preoccupied."

"No kidding."

For a while Mom just looks at me. She seems to be deciding something. Then she takes a deep breath.

"When I left Smallwood, your grandfather and I were not getting along ... at all."

"You left Gran too," I remind her.

"It wasn't an easy decision, Claire. But your grandmother, well, with the way things were between my father and me ... it was hard on her too. But she could live with him. I couldn't."

"Why not?"

Mom leans forward, her elbows on the table. "My father was a very rigid man. He lived by a set of rules and he expected everyone to do the same. It was fine when I was young, but as I grew up, he couldn't accept the fact that I had my own ideas

and didn't absolutely agree with him on everything."

"What kinds of things?"

"Church, for one," she says quickly. "My father
spent as much time churching as farming. We had
to go twice on Sundays; we attended midweek
programs, choir practice, prayer nights. It was
endless."

"It sounds exhausting," I say, but I can't help
thinking how similar it sounds to my piano and
sports commitments. "Did you hate it?"

"I just hated not being able to decide for myself.
I hated having it forced on me." She pours herself
another cup of coffee. "And then there was the
piano."

"Piano?"

"I loved it, Claire." Her voice is so low I have to
concentrate to make out the words. "Almost more
than anything. I think it was a way for me to say the
things I didn't even know I was feeling. It was my
voice." She looks away.

"Why did you stop?"

"Your grandfather decided that Sunday was not a
day for secular music. So unless I played hymns —
'sacred music' — I wasn't allowed to play at all."

Maybe I'm not quite getting it. How was this
different from all the times my mother made me
practice when I didn't feel like it? "But you could
play what you wanted the other six days, right?"

The look on her face makes me sorry I've said anything. Her eyes are so intense, it almost scares me. It's the same fury I saw when she found me with Jack.

"But you see, it was all on his terms. We'd have these arguments about what sacred music was. Didn't Bach qualify? Wasn't Beethoven holy enough? It was absurd to me, but he wouldn't give in, so I refused to play."

"That's why you stopped playing? You gave it up, just like that?"

"There were other reasons as well," she says shortly. "Anyway, Claire, I don't really want to get into this with you. It's got nothing to do with you and me. I just wanted you to know why I've been preoccupied, okay?"

"Okay."

But it's not okay. What happened between her and her father had everything to do with us.

13

I decide to walk down to the brook to organize the thoughts that are tumbling around in my head. Doing somersaults and back flips, actually. The air has a freshly scrubbed smell from the rain and the clouds have cleared, the storm passing over to somewhere beyond the mountains. The twilight sky is changing from a deep, sharp blue to soft, filmy mauve. The blurred, grainy atmosphere matches my mood as I walk along the curving path.

The talk I had with Mom proves how different we are. I wonder if I'll ever really understand her. For her, church was a prison. I felt peaceful there. She saw rules as a personal challenge. I almost never bothered to question them. She loved the craziness of the city. I was falling in love with the slower rhythm of the country.

Maybe parents and kids are supposed to drive each other crazy ... maybe it's written in the DNA.

A blue heron is standing in the middle of the slow-moving water, so I approach cautiously. I expect the

large bird to fly away, but as I sit down on my rock —
still damp from the rain — it remains motionless
except for a dip of its regal head to drink from the
brook. Then it raises its beak and looks deeply into
my eyes. I smile at it.

"There's a legend around here," someone says.
I turn and see Mac, like an apparition in the dusky
evening. "If you hold the gaze of a heron long
enough, eventually it will speak to you." His voice
is deeper than I remembered, and I want him to
keep talking so I can memorize it for when he
disappears again.

"Really?" I take a quick peek back at the heron,
but my voice scares it. With a lurch of its broad
wings, it squawks and clumsily takes flight.

Mac sits on a log beside the water. He dips his
hand into it, letting the stream find its way around
his fingers. "No, not really. But people around here
are always coming up with stories and sayings.
I thought I'd give it a try."

I smile at him uncertainly. I can't tell if he's
joking or not. After wondering about him all my
life, here we are having a conversation about
talking birds. "That's funny," I say, for lack of
anything more profound.

"How've you been?" he asks.

Does he mean how am I right now or how have
I been for my whole entire life? I decide he means

right now. "Good, thanks. I, um, really like it here. On the farm, I mean."

"That's nice. Funny in a way, though."

"Why funny?"

"Your mother hated — well, hate is probably too strong a word for it — disliked farm life."

"Gran says Mom's a city gal."

"City gal." Mac's eyes have a faraway look. I wonder who he's seeing. Me or my mom.

"What was she like?" I ask abruptly, to jar him out of his dream state.

"Your mother?" He takes some time before he answers. "You know the way a sunrise looks, all orange and pink and purple, before it finally gives up the color to the blue?"

I nod.

"That was your mother, except she never gave way to the blue. Never. At least, not when I knew her."

I blink back a sudden prickling of tears. I've never seen this side of her.

I can't think of a thing to say. He was always such a perfect fantasy, but I don't know where to begin with an actual father.

What right does he have after fifteen years of nothing to make me feel anything? I can tell my face is freezing over like a pond in wintertime. Good, I think. Frozen is good.

"This must be difficult for you," Mac says, watching me closely. "Walking back into your mother's past."

I peer at him through icy eyes. "I don't know very much about my mom's past," I say, pitching a rock across to the other bank. "She doesn't talk about the old days."

"She was always looking ahead, that's for sure. Your mother had so many dreams and ambitions. I never could keep up with her. She used to tell me that I could be anything I wanted. I just needed to believe in myself." He smiles and his face crinkles around the eyes. "I told her she should be a motivational speaker."

I smile as I remember all her piano, soccer and dance speeches: "Hard work, Claire. It comes down to that."

"She never quite understood that some people weren't born to sprint. I was always more of a stroller, I think."

"Me too," I say, moving a little closer. Just to get a better look, I tell myself.

"Clarissa, I didn't run into you by accident. Now, today, I mean. I was going to the farmhouse when I saw you walk toward the woods, so I took a chance you were coming here."

"You were looking for me?" The muscles in my stomach tighten.

"I'm not trying to go behind your mother's back. She made her feelings pretty clear the other day, but I wanted to see you — to explain."

I wait. My feelings are so jumbled up, I couldn't explain anything.

Mac moves to the edge of the water, peering down at his reflection. "Do you know that you look like me a bit?"

"It's the five o'clock shadow."

He chuckles and shakes his head. "I was thinking more of my nose and hair."

"Oh, that." I touch my own hair self-consciously. "I've always liked my hair."

He sits back down on the log and takes a deep breath. "You know, when your mother told me she was pregnant, I couldn't believe it. I mean, it's a cliché, I guess, the thing men always say. But truly, I couldn't grasp the fact. We were both so innocent."

"Innocent? I do know how babies are made."

He smiles a half smile. I think to myself, I could get used to that. "Fair enough. But it wasn't planned — none of it. It was just this one time. Your mother was in a ... I don't know, particularly orange and purple mood over something at home and ... it just happened. Later, when she told me she was pregnant, I couldn't connect the two events. She looked the same, I was the same, yet everything had changed." He looks at me sadly. "I was your mother's best friend, Clarissa. And when she looked to me for help, I let her down."

"But what about the baby you made? Weren't you even curious?" My voice has an edge to it. I sound like my mother. "What about me?"

Mac looks puzzled, but gradually his eyes change. "My letters. You never got them." It's a statement, not a question.

The significance hits me: he *had* tried to contact me. She had stopped him.

"No, I didn't."

"Listen, Clarissa, I don't want to stir things up between you and your mother. She's obviously done a fine job raising you. I guess she didn't think I deserved a second chance and maybe I didn't. But that's not why I'm here."

"Why are you here then?"

"I wanted you to know that I don't hold it against you — or your mother."

I don't know what I expected to hear, but this isn't it.

"That's big of you." I hurl the words at him. "Do you want me to apologize for being born?"

Mac looks as if I've slapped him. "Of course not. I'm talking about the other day when I spoke with your mother."

I try to remember what Mom had said. "She told me you asked for a favor and then left."

Mac looks like he's fighting for control. "That's all she told you?"

I try to recall anything else, but there's nothing. "Yes. Why?"

He doesn't answer, and I can't stand it. This can't turn into another dead-end secret. "Tell me. Please."

"The other day? I wanted to talk to your mother about letting me have contact with you. But she was right, I also had a favor to ask."

"Of me?"

Mac nods. "I'm not sure you know — my son has been very ill."

Jamie. I hadn't even thought to ask about him. "Yes, Gran told me. How is he? I really like him."

A smile transforms Mac's face. "Well, he's madly in love with you. He's convinced you're a forest princess." He rubs his neck, the smile fading. "But he's not well. They've tried all the conventional treatments but the, the ... cancer is back." His voice chokes up. Tiny veins are pulsating on the side of his neck.

"I'm sorry," I whisper.

For a while neither of us speaks. I want to touch his hand, but I don't dare.

"There's a chance that if he has a bone marrow transplant, he'll be able to beat this thing."

I look at him, not understanding what all this has to do with a favor.

"They haven't been able to find a compatible donor. His mother and I have been tested. So have other relatives, but there hasn't been a match. His best chance, however slight, is with a relative."

I feel ridiculous for not figuring it out before. "Me?"

When he takes my hand, his skin feels warm and slightly rough. "It would be difficult for him, but not for the donor. Otherwise I wouldn't ask. I know that I have no right, but ..."

"I'll be tested."

He looks surprised at my quick answer. "You need to give this some thought, Clarissa."

"No, I don't. What's to think about? Some things you just know."

His eyes fill with tears. Then he gets up slowly and hugs me. Exactly the way I've imagined it so many times.

"Thank you."

We walk back to the farmhouse together. There are still a thousand things I want to ask him, but I've wanted a father for so long, I can't quite believe he won't just disappear.

I can feel my insides churn as I think about Mom. But I'm not nervous about telling her my decision. I'm furious with her for keeping the truth from me — again.

"I'll come with you," he says, and I nod.

But when we reach the driveway, I see her car

is gone. Gran's sitting on the porch drinking a cup of tea.

"It's good to see you, Mac." Gran doesn't seem particularly surprised to find us together.

"Where's Mom?" I ask. "I need to talk to her."

"She went for a drive. Didn't say when she'd be back. Is everything all right?"

"It will be," I say, looking at Mac. "I'll talk to her," I promise.

"Can you stay for tea?" Gran asks.

Mac shakes his head. "I have to get back to the hospital. Jamie will be driving the nurses crazy by now. Yesterday he took off with his I.V. stand. They found him on the maternity ward hunting dragons."

"Alonzo the Fearsome?" I guess, and Mac laughs, nodding.

"I better get going," he says.

I walk with him to the end of the driveway. He tells me a few more "Jamie and the dragon" stories, but I hear only every other word. I'm still trying to get used to him being this close. He tells me which hospital Jamie is at, and I repeat my promise to go to Vancouver for the test. He gives me a quick hug and continues walking up the road toward his farm. I watch until he's a blurry, distant figure.

When I return to the porch, Gran looks at me curiously, but as much as I want to talk to someone, I'm too angry to do it now.

"I'm going to turn in early, Gran."

She seems disappointed, but nods and gives me a kiss.

I close the bedroom door firmly and walk up to the desk. Without a second thought, I pull open the drawer and take out my mother's diary.

I begin to read.

14

April 2

Dear Diary:

Mac and I went fishing this morning at 5:30. It was still dark outside but he was determined to see the sun rise — like he hasn't seen it rise a billion times before. I wanted to stay in bed but he was throwing rocks at my window — who could sleep? Finally I gave in. But justice prevailed — I caught three trout, he caught nothing. He whined about it, so I gave him one but made him clean them all ...

Janey

Sounds like Mom all right, a good deal maker even then. I flip over a couple of pages, anxious to find out more. I feel the tiniest twinge of guilt, but ignore it.

April 11

Dear Di:

Ruth and I talked Dad into letting us go
with him to Vancouver today. We told him
we had to use the library for a research
project. For three glorious hours I was free.
We walked around downtown and ate
sundaes and bought red lipstick. It was
marvelous. Ruth says the tall buildings freak
her out but I loved them. I'm going to live
in one of those buildings one day. I'll be a
concert pianist — Mr. Harms says I'm good
enough — and I'll travel the world. I can't
wait.

Barely waiting,
Janey

My heart is pounding. The words sound so
young and hopeful, so full of dreams — not like
my practical, hard-driving mother. I want to read
every page, but I'm looking for a clue that will
reveal why my mother has turned so tough inside.
I want to find out when she became the person
who would say no to a little boy's last chance.

May 5

Di:

There's no pleasing him. It doesn't matter what I do, how hard I work, how often I sit in that depressing church listening to boring sermons. It's never enough. Tonight he was "disappointed" that I was laughing in church. I asked him if God didn't have a sense of humor and he sent me to my room! He still treats me like a child.

I know he used to take me on tractor rides and have hay fights in the barn with me, but I can hardly remember. Sometimes I think that must have been another father ... another life.

Jane

I close the diary. I don't feel like reading more. I'm feeling sorry for this girl, and sympathy is the last thing I want to feel right now.

I walk around the room a couple of times, eyeing the small book on the bed. Then I pick it up again. This time I open it much farther on.

November 5

Dear Diary:

He's really done it this time. He told me I can't play my music on Sundays unless it's from the hymnal. Who does he think he is? God's personal music critic?

I'll die here, I know it. Sometimes I feel like I can't even breathe, like the walls are closing in on me. Mom's no help. I know she doesn't care what I play as long as I play. Why won't she say anything?

It's 7:00 in the evening. I made Mac promise to come for me at midnight. He thinks I'm crazy, but he promised.

I have to get away from here ...

J.

November 6

Di:

Mac and I did something really stupid last night. He didn't even really want to do it. He said we should wait. I can't write it, what if someone ever reads this? It would kill Daddy if he knew.

It wasn't the way I thought it would be.

Mac was scared, I was nervous, and it hurt. I
didn't know it would hurt. What have I
done?

I turn the page, not wanting to read any more,
but I have to know. I feel sick for my mother, and
tears are rolling down my face as I uncover the
moment I was conceived. But when I turn the
page, it's empty. I keep flipping — page after page
of white, empty paper. Finally I reach a page with
two lines written on it.

December

It's over. God help me.

The rest of the book reveals only untouched
pages.

I tuck the book back into the drawer as far as it
will go and push it shut.

I hear a noise behind me. Mom is standing just
inside the room, her hand gripping the doorknob
for support, it looks like. We look at each other for
what feels like an eternity, but then she roughly
pulls the drawer open and grabs the diary. Her
hands are shaking and her face is blotchy with rage.

"Mom," I begin, my voice cracking.

"Don't. Not now." She holds the book
protectively under her arm and leaves.

I don't know how long I sit on the bed. I try to decide what to do next, but my mind is a mass of confused images. I feel so alone. Finally, I try to pray, even though it's kind of unfamiliar. The only thing I say is "God help me." Then I fall into a dark, dreamless sleep.

Sometime later, I wake to a spray of noise. I'm still in my clothes and it's dark outside. I look at the alarm clock. Four-thirty. I turn over and try to get back to sleep.

Then I hear a tapping coming from the window-pane. I walk over and pull the window open. There, practically in my face, stands — or rather clings — Jack, perilously holding on to the trellis. I open my mouth to scream, but he covers it with his hand — and almost falls.

"What are you doing?" I hiss, grabbing his hand until he is stable again.

"Whew, that was close," he says, looking down at the ground, then back at me with a crooked grin. "Hey, Juliet, Juliet ... wherefore art thou ... oh, forget it. Want to see a calf being born?"

I try to register his words, since I'm still groggy.

"What?" The word comes out sharply.

"C'mon, city girl," he says. He holds out his hand, but almost loses his balance again.

I wait until he's steadied himself. "I'll take the stairs like a normal human being." I know he won't give up. Besides, I'm awake now.

"Sure, take the easy way." He climbs down the trellis and lands with a muffled thump against the siding.

I walk quietly through the house. If my mother catches me sneaking out, I'll be in three more kinds of trouble.

I close the screen door carefully behind me.

"You're crazy," I accuse Jack in a loud whisper.

"No, it's great. You're gonna love this." He grabs my hand and pulls me through the dewy grass to the barn.

I'm breathless and my feet are sopping wet. Smells of grain and cow manure and fresh straw mix in the chilly night air. From the corner of the barn I hear a low moan.

"If my mom catches us, we're dead," I warn.

But Jack's face is all business now.

"Come up to the stall, but then don't move. We don't want to scare her."

I peer over the low door as he walks slowly to the stall, toward the heaving animal. She looks at him with huge trusting eyes. Her belly is convulsing with contractions, and her sides are straining, it seems, to the point of bursting.

"Is she okay?"

"Sure," Jack says softly. "She's been through this before, right, Marcia?" Jack strokes her evenly, gently. Mom told me that when I was born she'd been scared out of her mind. Maybe if she'd had someone's soothing hands on her ...

Jack sits there for a long time and I watch, mesmerized by the hypnotic rhythm, by the enormity of what is happening. Marcia is trying to push new life into the world. I wonder if the calf is pulling just as hard to stay inside where it's warm and familiar. Then the animal becomes agitated and Jack jumps to his feet. He slips on a glove and moves to Marcia's back end. I guess I should have paid more attention in sex education class, because when he reaches inside — like, right inside the animal — I gasp.

"It's close," Jack mutters between gritted teeth. "Grab that rope over there," he orders, pointing to a coil hanging on a hook beside the stable door.

I do as I'm told, handing it to him nervously, not wanting to get too close.

"Grab her tail and hold it up."

"Huh?" My mind is having trouble registering the fact that he expects me to touch this huge heaving animal.

"It's okay." Jack's eyes are reassuring.

I carefully pluck at the swishing tail like it's a day-old fish.

"She's got other things on her mind, Claire. Just grab it, okay? You're helping her."

I hold it firmly then, and suddenly feel that I am a small part of the process.

Two small hooves are now showing. Jack grabs them, wrapping the rope around them. "C'mon, baby. Push, baby. You can do it," he says over and over again like a chant.

Marcia closes her eyes, her bulky body shaking and straining. The muscles on Jack's face contort as he pulls on the newborn calf. With a slippery lurch, the tiny animal plops, along with a pool of slick blood and mucus, onto the bed of straw.

There is suddenly a sour stench, but I don't care, although I do have the presence of mind to let go of the tail. Jack unwraps the rope from the calf and crawls backward like a scuttling crab to the corner of the stall. We stand there, awed. Jack is breathing heavily from the exertion.

"Wow," I say.

The mother begins to lick at the calf's face. Suddenly the little guy sucks in air greedily — his first breath of life. My knees buckle and I hold on to the wall for support. Tears are running down my face.

"Pretty cool, huh?" Jack says, scrambling to his feet. He returns to the cow and helps her deliver what I think at first must be another calf, but he pulls a slimy glob of tissue from her body instead. It must be the afterbirth. Jack's covered up to his elbows in blood and guck.

"Wow and yuck," I say.

Jack laughs. "Yup, that's it. Wow and yuck."

After he's cleaned up the mess in the stall, he walks over to where I'm standing and hoists himself up on the ledge of the stable door. We both watch as the calf and mother get to know each other. Marcia licks away the yellow mucus from her calf, and he closes his eyes.

"You don't want to get too close to her now. That protection thing can get pretty intense," he says, still watching the animals.

"I guess that's the way it works."

Jack peels his overalls off to his jeans and T-shirt beneath. Then he walks over to the sink and washes up.

"How did you know it would happen tonight?"

He shrugs. "Just a feeling. So, now you have something to write Rtodd about."

My euphoria slips away.

"There's no Rtodd, Jack."

"I know, it's Todd." He says the name with exaggerated emphasis.

"No." I look him full in the face. "I mean, there's no boyfriend. I lied. I don't know why. It just slipped out and then I didn't know how to ..." My voice fades to nothing. Jack looks away.

"I'm sorry," I mumble.

"It's okay." He shrugs.

But it's not. Jack looks hurt and embarrassed, and I feel sick.

Our closeness seems gone forever now.

Jack tries to smile, but it doesn't reach his eyes. "I've been rejected before but as far as I know, no one has ever created a fictitious person to avoid me. This is definitely a first."

I try to touch his arm but he walks past me to the stall, where the mother and baby are lying together peacefully.

"So why didn't you just say you weren't interested?" he asks, without looking at me.

"Because I was," I admit.

He looks at me sideways. "So who does that make you, opposite girl?"

I laugh, relieved at the touch of friendliness in his voice. "Not really. Usually I'm pretty straight-forward. Maybe I was afraid to let you get too close," I say, feeling the risk of my words. "It kinda runs in my family."

"Ah," he nods wisely. "So it's a genetic thing."

"I guess. Forgive me?"

"I'll consider it."

"Good, because I have a favor to ask you."

"Let me get this straight," he says, slipping his arms into his jacket. "First you try to drown me, then you assault me. Now I find out you've been living a gruesome lie involving a phony preppie football-playing boyfriend who left me looking like a total farmboy loser, and now you want me to do you a favor?"

"Maybe I prefer farmboy losers," I say quietly.

He brightens a little at this. "Well, in that case, what's the favor?"

"I need a lift somewhere."

"When?"

Not why or where. Just "when?"

I look at my watch in the dim light. It's five thirty and the darkness is just beginning to recede. "Right now."

"Let's go."

I write a note and leave it on the kitchen table.

> I've gone for a ride with Jack. I'll be fine.
> I'll be home before supper.
>
> Clarissa

I close the door carefully and run to Jack's truck. He has the motor running.

"Where to?" he asks when I climb inside.

"Children's Hospital. You know where it is?"

"Vancouver," he says, and we start up the road. The sun is just peeking over the mountains. The sky is bright, bright orange.

15

We stop about halfway to the hospital for breakfast. In the rush, I forgot to bring money, so I pretend I'm not hungry; but Jack insists on buying hash browns and orange juice for me.

"I'll pay you back later," I promise.

"Forget it."

"You're being too nice to me," I complain. "You're making me feel even worse about lying to you before."

"That's the idea," he says, without looking at me. He turns back onto the highway, his orange juice between his knees. The sky is pale blue now, the earlier brilliance tucked away behind the mountains. Commuter traffic is clogging the highway, and we crawl toward town.

"So you're going to kill me with kindness?" I munch the hash browns eagerly, hungrier than I thought.

"You know, you're very attractive when you talk with your mouth full," he observes out of the corner of his eye. I make a face at him and take a large gulp of orange juice.

"Why do you want to go to the hospital?" he asks. Finally.

"Mac came to see me yesterday. You know Jamie is sick? Well, he needs a bone marrow transplant and I'm going to find out if I'm a possible donor."

Jack lets out a protracted whistle. "Will it hurt?"

"I don't think so. I hadn't really thought about it. Thanks for mentioning it, though."

"Well, it's nice you want to help."

"You'd do the same thing," I say, remembering how gentle he'd been with Marcia.

"I guess," he agreed thoughtfully. "Who wouldn't help a little kid?"

"My mother," I say softly.

~ ~ ~

It's almost eight o'clock by the time we reach the hospital. Jack lets me out at the front door and goes to park the truck. I guess I expected the hospital to be institutional, depressing, but it looks more like an enchanted forest: supporting beams disguised as tall fir trees, elevators pretending to be woodsy bungalows, and brightly painted forest creatures covering the walls.

I spot the information desk, an island of reality.

"Hi," I say. A woman is just sitting down with a cup of coffee. "Could you tell me which room Jamie McGregor is in?"

"Visiting hours begin at nine o'clock," she says.

"I'm here to take a test, a bone marrow compatibility test, I think."

"Oh." She gives me the room number with a smile. "The lab is on the second floor. His room is on the third." She gives me instructions to both places, and I try to keep them straight.

"Thanks." I wait for Jack.

There's something about the air in a hospital, no matter how the hospital is decorated. I'm sure it's thinner than normal — you have to breathe twice as hard to get the same amount of oxygen.

When I look through the small glass square on Jamie's door, I can see he's still sound asleep. His blond hair, cropped short, stands up straight from his head, and his skin is the color of the pillow. In the corner, Mac is asleep in a dark green vinyl chair, his head bent awkwardly against the wall.

It's probably the lack of sleep, but I feel like crying. Jack seems to understand.

"People always look gray in hospital beds. It's the way they do their laundry or something ... I read a study on it," he adds weakly.

I poke him in the ribs. "Thanks anyway. C'mon, let's go find the lab."

It takes us a full fifteen minutes to find it, and when we finally arrive, the door is locked.

I lean against the door. I was so sure I was going to whistle in and save the day. Now I'm starting to wonder: maybe I just want to be the hero so that Mac won't be able to resist loving me.

"Hey, don't look so discouraged. Someone will show up. We did sort of get an early start."

I slump down to sit on the floor. Jack sits against the opposite wall. His outline is a welcome relief against the knowledge that we're not in an enchanted forest after all.

"Did you ever do something good, but your reasons were totally selfish? Or at least partly?" I ask.

"Sure." Jack scratches his head. "What's wrong with that, as long as you still do it?"

"Nothing, I guess. I was just wondering if you can ever totally understand why people do things. Like with my grandfather. He sounds pretty selfish, but maybe he had reasons, too, you know, underneath the other reasons for doing some of the things he did."

"I remember your grandfather," Jack says.

"What was he like?" I ask nervously.

Jack considers the question. Finally he says, "I don't really know."

"You don't know?"

"He seemed like a decent guy. He was a real hard worker and super involved in the church. He had

this beard, you know? I used to think he looked like
Moses when I was a little kid."

"Moses. The guy who brought down the Ten
Commandments?"

"Yup. But I didn't know him really. Like, I never
heard him laugh."

"Never?"

"Not once."

I think of Gran's easy smile and fits of
uncontrolled laughter. "I bet Gran made him
laugh," I say, wanting it to be true.

"I'm sure she did," Jack says, but he doesn't
sound convinced.

A nurse is padding up the hall toward us. I
scramble away from the door. She slows as she
reaches us, taking out a large key chain. "Can I help
you?" she asks as she opens the door.

"Yes. I'm here to take a bone marrow test, or
something like that. It's for Jamie McGregor ... my
brother." The word "brother" stumbles off my tongue.

The nurse lets us into the room. "Do you have an
appointment?" she asks.

"Uh," I say stupidly. I hadn't even thought about
an appointment. "No, I don't."

She looks at me over her half glasses. "Well, let's
take a look here." She clicks on her computer and
scans the screen. Jack gives me a thumbs up, and I
feel slightly encouraged. "They've tested a lot of
people," I blurt. "And, um ..."

"Here he is. Uh-huh," she watches the screen with a concerned look. "Let me see if I can reach Dr. Fielding. Why don't you fill out the forms, and I'll let you know when I'm ready for you."

She passes me a long sheet of paper on a clipboard. Name, address, date of birth ... all the regular stuff. Then, at the bottom of the form, "Parent's or guardian's signature, if a minor." I get up and walk back to the counter.

"Oh, excuse me, Nurse ..." I look down at the tag pinned to her uniform. It reads "Alison Rambo, R.N." I suppress the urge to giggle nervously.

"Is this parent's signature really necessary? I mean, it's for my brother, right?"

Nurse Rambo gives me a half smile.

"It's just that she's out in Smallwood, and it's a long trip for a signature."

"What about your father?"

Mac. Of course. "Good thinking. I'll be right back."

Jamie is still asleep but Mac's chair is empty.

"He's not ..." I start to say, but then I see Mac heading toward us with a cup of coffee.

He looks surprised to see us and checks his watch. "Boy, you must have had an early start. Thanks, Clarissa." He smiles at Jack.

"Oh, this is Jack Peterson ... and Mac McGregor," I say quickly.

Mac holds out his hand and shakes Jack's hand. "You're Tom Peterson's boy, right?"

Jack nods. "That's right."

"We went to high school together," he says, taking a sip of coffee.

I must have looked surprised because Mac adds, "There's only one high school in Smallwood, Clarissa."

I hold the form out to Mac. "I need the signature of, um, a parent, before I can be tested."

Mac looks over the sheet carefully. "Your mother should really sign this. You have talked to her about being tested, haven't you?"

"Oh, yeah." I am not about to let my mother get in the way of helping Jamie. "It's just that I got a ride up with Jack, and we completely forgot about the permission thing." I glance over: Jack is leaning against the wall, looking away from us. He probably thinks that lying is a total way of life for me.

"Well, as long as you've discussed this with her." He puts down his coffee and signs the sheet. "How did you change her mind?"

"You know," I say, since I'm not really up for any more lying. "The nurse is waiting for this form, so I better go, okay? I'll come back when it's over."

Jack doesn't say anything as we walk back to the lab, but I know what he's thinking.

"I'll tell him," I say. "I will."

"What if the bone marrow matches and your mother won't let you do it?"

"I can't think of that right now. Besides, Mac could sign for that too."

At the lab, the nurse says that the test has been approved. She ushers me into a small sterile room. I say good-bye to Jack, trying to sound confident even though I'm not. The testing isn't as simple as I thought: there will be a blood test, X rays and then a sample of the bone marrow. Nurse Rambo tells me there will be some discomfort involved in taking the sample. "Discomfort." The medical code word for pain. I briefly consider chickening out, but then I think of Jamie and roll up my sleeve.

As Nurse Rambo prepares the needle and the vials for my blood, I flash back to every mad-scientist horror film I've ever seen and I look away. Jack is just outside the door — the thought calms me a little. I feel the needle pressing into the soft skin of the crook of my arm and hold my breath.

"It's better to breathe, dear." The nurse says evenly.

The X rays are even less fun. I have to take off my clothes, put on a paper gown, and wait in a little cubicle. The grim technician doesn't even smile as she takes me to the X-ray room. She looks as though she could use a good laugh, but I'm in no mood to tell jokes. She tells me to lie on a cold metal table, places my limbs in totally unnatural positions, and orders me not to move.

Suddenly I want my mother to be here — to hold my hand and tell me everything will be all right. Instead, I try to concentrate on the fact that I'm still wearing my own socks. I stare at them until the pictures have been taken.

Next is the bone marrow biopsy. Biopsy. Even the word sounds frightening. Dr. Fielding explains what she's going to do, but all I hear is that she will have to medicate me. I agree with this idea completely.

"Would you like me to ask your friend to come in here with you?" she asks.

I shake my head. "I'll be okay." As nervous as I am, this is my decision now — my choice — and I need to go through it alone. I wonder if I'm trying to prove something. But then the medication kicks in and I float away.

When I come to, I feel like my eyelids are being held down by tent pegs.

I hear Nurse Rambo talking to Jack in the next room, and I'm relieved to know the procedure is over. One by one, the tent pegs spring free. I slowly open my eyes and lift my gown to look at a bandage on my hip. Its smallness surprises me.

"You can wait for her if you want," Nurse Rambo is saying. "She'll be a little light-headed. I want her to sit still until she feels strong."

I quickly pull the gown down over my leg and yank a blanket across the bottom half of my body.

Jack's head appears in the doorway. It takes me a second to realize that the rest of his body is following. "How's it going?" His voice is the same one he used for Marcia.

"I feel like I just had a calf," I say groggily. I don't recognize my voice. My throat feels like it's got a wad of cotton in it. I smile goofily at him.

"I don't think that's scientifically possible," he says seriously.

I can't keep the stupid smile off my face. It's so nice to see him after all those strangers poking and prodding. "Thanks for coming here today with me," I gush. "And for letting me see the calf being born. And the other day at the river ..." I take a drink of water to see if it will dissolve the cotton. "I'm really sorry I lied to you about, well, you know." I have no control over my words. I put my hand on my head to keep it from floating away. "I feel weird."

"You are weird," Jack confirms. "Here, drink this juice. I think it helps." He sticks a bendable straw between my lips. I take a large gulp and begin to feel a little more attached to my body.

"Listen, Claire, I have to get to work. I'm late and ..."

"Oh." I put my hand over my mouth. It seems to take too long to get there. "I'm sorry, Jack. I didn't think ... I'm so selfish." I close my eyes. The room tilts just a little to the left.

Jack chuckles, a nice low sound. "I don't think this quite qualifies as selfish."

I feel like I've been given truth serum. "I don't know, Jack. I don't know why I'm doing this ... maybe it's for me. Maybe it's so Mac will notice me. And I'm still mad at my mom and I lied to Mac — about the permission thing." I open my eyes — there are two Jacks standing there. I blink a couple of times, and the two Jacks merge into one fuzzy person.

"Maybe you should put your head between your knees," Jack suggests.

I sit up straighter in the bed. "Why?"

"I don't know," he shrugs. "That's what they told us to do when we were donating blood."

I lean forward, and it seems to help. Gradually the room slows down. I look at Jack sheepishly.

"You probably think I'm a little strange, don't you?"

Jack shakes his head. "We passed 'a little strange' a while ago. It's one of the things I like about you."

I want to ask him what else he likes, except the truth-serum effect is wearing off.

"Can I just say hello to Jamie before we go back? Two minutes."

"Sure."

When I'm feeling strong enough to get out of bed, I shoo Jack out of the room. I put each article of clothing on carefully, relieved that I've worn loose-fitting shorts as I gingerly pull them over the bandage.

I catch my reflection beside the door. My skin is paler than usual — must be the medication — but I look familiar, more familiar than I've ever looked in my life.

16

After we check out with the nurse — results within two weeks — we go to find Jamie.

His room is painted sunshine yellow, and there are sketches of woodland creatures peering cheekily down from the walls.

Jamie is awake, sitting up in bed.

"Lady Guinevere!" he squeals. He looks less pale than he did while he was sleeping.

I sit on the edge of his bed. "How are you feeling?"

He scowls back at me. "Everybody asks me that. I want to go home." He leans forward and whispers. "Will you help me escape?"

Mac walks into the room carrying a tray of food. "There will be no escapes, young man," he says sternly, but his eyes are smiling at me. "How'd it go?" he asks.

"They'll know in a couple of weeks."

He nods. Of course. He's been through this before.

"Who's that?" Jamie blurts out, pointing to Jack.

"This is a friend of mine. His name's Jack. He delivered a calf this morning."

"Cool," Jamie says admiringly. Jack comes over to the bed and gives Jamie a high five.

"I hear you chase dragons," he says seriously.

Jamie shrugs his shoulders. "Sometimes." He looks at me. "Is he your boyfriend?"

I blush at the unexpected question but Jack's no help. He just smiles.

Fortunately Mac comes to the rescue. "Here, Mr. Nosy. It's time to eat your breakfast."

Jack looks at his watch. I get up from the bed. "I guess we should be going. Jack has to go to work," I say reluctantly.

"Already? You just got here!"

"I know." I'm disappointed, too, but I can't keep Jack any longer. "I'm sorry."

"I could give you a ride back later if you'd like," Mac offers. "There are a few things I need to do at the farm."

"I could let your mother know," Jack says, reading my mind.

My mother will have two fits, I decide, but when I look at Jamie's hopeful face, I have to stay.

"Good idea," I say to Jack. "I'll walk you out. And, Jamie, you finish your breakfast. I'll be right back."

Jamie tears off a chunk of toast with his small front teeth, nodding.

"What should I tell her?" Jack asks as we move into the bright morning sunshine. The breeze on my face feels welcome after the unnatural forced air in the hospital.

"Tell her I'm doing a favor for someone," I say, then quickly change my mind. "No, never mind. Just tell her I'm at the hospital and that I'll explain when I get home."

"Okay. So, I'll see you ..." Jack looks awkward, and suddenly I feel shy with him.

"Yeah, see you." I watch as he walks toward his truck. "Wait, Jack."

He stops and I catch up to him. "Thanks, really, for bringing me." And then, without even thinking, I reach up and kiss him lightly on the lips. I can't believe I've done it. I move back a step, embarrassed. He pulls his cap out from his back pocket and places it on his head.

"You're blushing," I can't resist adding.

"I'm sensitive to the sun," he says gruffly, but he's smiling as he walks to his truck.

Jamie has finished his breakfast by the time I return. A nurse is taking some blood. When she finishes, he rubs his arm but doesn't complain. The bruises up and down his arm make my insides twist.

"You take it easy today, James," the nurse warns seriously. "No running around the halls."

"Yes Sir, Ma'am." He gives her a salute. He doesn't really look capable of running anywhere.

The nurse smiles kindly at him, and as she leaves, I think I see a sparkle of tears in her eyes. He must be doing worse than I thought.

"Daddy says you're my sister!" he announces suddenly, leaning back into his pillow.

I sit in a chair next to the bed and look over to Mac.

"I thought he should know," Mac explains. "I hope that's okay?"

I nod. "Of course. So what do you think about that?" I ask Jamie.

The little boy shrugs. "Can brothers and sisters get married?"

I smile at this. Mac chuckles. "I knew he was in love with you," he says, ruffling Jamie's cap of hair.

"Dad!" the little boy protests, embarrassed. "That's not what I meant," he assures me. "Mallory Spatman has a new boyfriend every recess and lunch."

I try to remember what it is like to be seven years old, when every subject is connected by invisible thread. "Oh really? Were you ever her boyfriend?"

He shakes his head energetically. "No, but I was on a list once."

I struggle not to laugh as Mac suddenly disappears behind a magazine.

"So you don't have a girlfriend?"

"Nope," Jamie says. "I'm too young."

"Just girls who are friends?"

Jamie considers the question. "There are four girls in my class who don't bug me too much. And Jennifer."

"Jennifer?"

"Jennifer, next door. She's sick, too." He says this matter-of-factly.

"They've already gotten into a certain amount of trouble together," Mac says.

I walk over to the window. Jamie's room overlooks the parking lot and the busy streets beyond. It feels strange to be back in a city after the peace of the country.

Jamie watches me closely. "My friend Bud and me are blood brothers. We got this pin and poked our fingers? Blood squirted everywhere," he gestures wildly around the room. "And when we mushed it together we said ..." He stops suddenly. "Oh, I can't tell you. It's a secret."

"That's okay. Some secrets are okay."

"Do you want to?" he asks.

"Do I want to what?"

"You know, be blood brothers? Or blood sister and brother?" He points to the bandages we're both wearing in the crook of our arm.

I look over his head and meet Mac's eyes. "I hope so."

After we've played so many games of Crazy Eights that I've lost count, Jamie's eyelids start to droop and Mac suggests a nap. Jamie resists, but within moments he's fast asleep.

"Let's go to the cafeteria and get something to eat," Mac whispers.

I look down at my watch. It's one thirty. The morning has slipped by so quickly that I haven't even noticed I've missed lunch.

We pick a table near the back of the room and sit down with our food. For a while we just eat in silence. The food isn't great, but I'm hungry.

Mac sips his coffee. "So tell me about your conversation with Janey."

The sudden bluntness takes me by surprise.

"I didn't tell her," I say simply.

"How come?"

I'm relieved that he doesn't seem angry. "I was going to tell her last night," I say. Was it really only last night? "But she wasn't home — and then I did something that made her so furious I couldn't bring it up — and then I just decided to come." I add defensively, "It's my bone marrow."

"What did you do that made her so furious?"

I take a deep breath. "I found her diary and started reading it. I wasn't going to," I blurt. "When I first found it in the drawer, I left it — but last night it seemed the only way I could understand her, you know?"

Mac leans back in the chair. "Oh, I know." He sounds so sad that I feel angry all over again at the way my mother runs people's lives.

"She has to have everything her own way. She decided for me that I shouldn't know you or my grandfather and even my grandmother for most of my life. I feel like a prisoner, like she's kept me all for herself. All these years I felt responsible for ruining her life, but now — I'm sick of it."

"She probably thought she was protecting you."

"Protecting me? From what?" I say, too loudly. A couple of people turn to look at us. I lower my voice. "From who?" I add quietly.

Mac takes a gulp of coffee. "That's a tough question. You see your mother as a powerful person, I guess. But that's not the Janey I knew."

I wait for him to continue.

"Your mother was different from the other girls in Smallwood. She had such big dreams for her life ... we used to spend hours talking about how she would be a concert pianist and how we'd travel the world."

"You and her?" I ask.

"We planned to be together forever." The silence sits between us like a third person.

"And?" I urge softly, desperately not wanting the conversation to end here.

Mac doesn't even seem to know he's stopped talking and resumes without looking at me. "The morning she told me she was pregnant? She was so brave."

"Brave?" *I croak. It's over. God help me.* That was brave?

"She was scared at first. Of course. We both were. But then she came up with a whole new dream. We'd get married and raise you together. We'd work hard — she'd keep playing the piano ..." The words drift to silence again.

"But you didn't want that?"

"I could never say no to your mother, Clarissa. She was an amazing girl, just amazing." His voice falters but he keeps going. "We went to my parents with our plans. They were stunned. They couldn't believe I was considering getting married so young. I mean, they wanted me to do the right thing — marry her — but they wanted me to graduate first. I was only in grade eleven."

"Mom didn't want to wait?"

Mac hesitates. "She wanted to do this on our own ... without our parents' help. She needed to leave Smallwood. They — my parents — made her feel very responsible for what happened — and dirty. And I didn't stop them. I let them hurt her." Mac stops, his face full of pain.

Neither of us speaks for a while. When he begins again, his voice is stronger. "Her parents — your grandparents said they would raise you."

"My grandfather agreed?"

"Oh yes. He wouldn't have agreed to adoption — because of his own experience," he says.

I nod. " So why didn't Mom agree?" I ask. "It would have solved her problem."

Mac shakes his head, frowning. "No, it wouldn't. You were never the problem, Clarissa. For me, it was a problem. For my parents and for her parents, I think. But never for your mother. You were a miracle to her."

"But I ruined her life. All her plans!"

"She told me, the last day I saw her before she moved to Toronto, that she would never let anyone else raise you. She loved you from the beginning."

I shake my head. "No, maybe she felt responsible, but I read her diary, Mac. I know how much she wanted a different kind of life."

"Yes she did. And she gave it up — for you. She always said that becoming pregnant was her responsibility ... and mine. But it was never yours, Clarissa. Has she ever said you were a mistake — or that she resented you?"

"Not exactly. But it seemed so hard for her."

"Of course it was hard. There's nothing more difficult than raising a child alone. I know that ... now."

"Why didn't she accept any help?"

"We wanted — all of us — to help, at least financially, but like I said, your mother wanted to do it alone. She was stubborn as a mule, and I'm not saying she didn't make mistakes. She was a child in many ways. She wasn't much older than you are now."

I cough nervously, stealing a glance down at my reasonably flat stomach. I can't even imagine it.

"We all hurt her so deeply and let her down. Especially me. I don't think she ever got over it. But whatever she did, loving you was never in question."

I let the words penetrate my brain. Reasons under reasons, nothing as simple as it seems. I slump down in the chair, suddenly so tired. I can't finish my lunch.

"Are you all right?"

"I need to talk to her," I say quietly.

"I'll take you home."

We check on Jamie before we go. He cries when Mac tells him we're leaving. Mac takes Jamie's small body into his arms and holds him until the tears have stopped. I stand by the door watching, tears pouring down my own face.

"I'll be back before nighttime, okay? I'll put a video in for you and I'll be back before you know it." Mac's voice is strained, almost pleading, and I can feel his agony.

"Are you coming back?" Jamie looks up at me, his white face streaked with tears. He doesn't even bother trying to hide them from me.

I sit beside him on the bed and take his hand. "Would Lady Guinevere leave Sir Lancelot?"

"What about King Arthur?" he asks, unsure.

"Well, okay then. Would a sister leave her brother?"

Jamie still doesn't look convinced. "I don't know. I've never had a sister before."

"Well, I've never had a brother before either. Do you know what a miracle is, Jamie?"

The little boy nods. "Sure. It's, like, better than magic, right?"

I hug him. "Well, you're my miracle brother. And a person doesn't walk away from a miracle, okay?"

He looks satisfied at this. As we leave the room, I look back through the square of glass. He's not watching the video; he's watching us leave.

17

As we enter the house, I can hear Mom and Gran talking in low tones in the kitchen. I motion for Mac to follow me.

Gran sees us first. She looks relieved and concerned at the same time. Mom barely looks up. "You're back," she says. Her voice is lifeless.

Gran offers Mac a chair, but he moves over to my mother.

"I'm sorry, Janey. I thought Clarissa had spoken to you."

Mom doesn't respond. Then she gets up and walks right past him. "I need to speak to my daughter. Alone," she says pointedly and leads me to the music room. She closes the french doors behind us.

She makes a couple of attempts to speak but fails. Finally she manages, "How could you do this to me?"

"To you? Do what to you?"

"Go to Mac." She practically spits the words out.

"He's my father. His son is dying and there's a chance I can help." I can't believe she doesn't understand this.

"Don't be melodramatic, Claire. There are other treatments for leukemia. Ones that don't put you at risk."

I walk up to her so that we're face to face. "No, Mom, there aren't any other treatments for Jamie. It's his last chance. Did you know his name is Jamie? That he has blond hair like mine and that he likes to make up stories about knights and dragons?" I let the words sink in as I struggle to stay calm. "Were you ever going to tell me that Mac wanted me to be tested? Or were you just going to file it with all the other secrets?"

Mom's face has lost its color. She sits down on the chair.

"What secrets do you think I've been keeping?"

I can't believe this. There are too many to list: her father and their life together, Mac and their relationship. The possibilities fan out like a deck of cards. Pick a secret, any secret. But I answer, "You. You've kept yourself a secret."

I walk over to the window and look out. I can wait. When I move I can still feel the stiffness in my hip, and I know Mom has noticed my slight limp; she looks worried. But I don't want to think about that. I've been thinking about her worries all my life.

"I'm not doing this to hurt you, Mom," I say quietly.

Then there's a knock at the door and Mom looks startled by the sudden sound. It's Mac, looking in at us through the glass.

I open the door. He moves cautiously into the room.

"Janey, I'm sorry about today. There was a mis-understanding about the test. I wouldn't have ... I thought you had agreed."

"It's Jane, Mac," Mom says coldly, rising to her feet. "I am not the girl you grew up with, and I'd appreciate it if you would remember that. Claire is my daughter and my responsibility."

Mac holds out his arm as if he's trying to stop an oncoming train. "I know that, Janey. I mean, Jane. I'm not trying to take her away."

I feel like a piece of property. Of all the fantasies I've ever had about a reunion between my parents, this one has never come up.

"It's a remote chance she'll even be a match," he says softly.

"You said that the other day. So why did you push it, Mac? How dare you go behind my back. After all these years. You have no right!"

I find my voice. "He didn't go behind your back, Mother. He came to tell me that it was okay if I didn't want to be tested. For some strange reason, he assumed you had told me why he'd come.

Obviously he doesn't realize that you make all my decisions, so there was no need to tell me."

"I was trying to protect you, Claire," she says.

"I'm tired of being protected," I say, suddenly worn out. "I'm going to my room."

As I pass by Mac, he touches my shoulder. "Thank you, Claire. I'm grateful. It means a lot to me that you were willing to try."

I look at him squarely. "If my bone marrow matches, I will help Jamie."

My mother remains silent.

"I can't go against your mother's wishes," Mac says. I can see the strain on his face as he forces the words out.

"I won't let my brother die." I leave the room quickly. As angry as I am, I still can't let my mother see that, right now, at this moment, I hate her.

~ ~ ~

The following week goes on forever. There's a heat wave and the days stretch out, long and dull with no break from the dead August temperatures. Gran has fans in every room but they only move the sluggish air around.

I help Gran with the chores. Mom spends most of the time in her bedroom with a migraine. I know she's gone to some dark place inside herself, but I can't help her. I won't help her.

Without the smile I've grown to love, Gran seems older and more frail. It's the only thing that makes me question what I'm doing.

"Do you think I'm wrong, Gran?" I finally ask one day while we're picking apples off the birdhouse tree.

"You have to do what you think is right, Clarissa."

I'm so relieved that I want to cry, but I can't. A part of me has gone solid inside. Is this what happened to my mother? We finish picking in silence, but as we head back to the house, each holding one handle of the heavy apple-filled basket, a slight breeze — the first in a week — moves across the field, ruffling the tall grass in an almost straight line. We stop and let the wind blow over us, through us. I can hear chimes tinkling, and I see there are tears in my grandmother's eyes as she turns to look at the tall tree.

The wind dies down and we move slowly, without speaking, back to the house.

Inside, Gran and I gulp down huge glasses of iced tea. The phone rings. Gran moves to answer it but I'm closer.

"Is this Clarissa Harrison?" a strange voice inquires. My heart is pounding. "This is Dr. Fielding. We have the test results. The marrow is a good match." A tingle in my toes becomes an electrical current throughout my body. "It's quite remarkable," she adds almost primly.

I miss some of what the doctor is saying, but I force myself to pay attention while I grab a chair ... before my knees give way.

"We'll need to admit you in ten days. Will that be possible?"

I nod emphatically before I remember that I'm on the phone. "Yes, I'll be there."

Even after the connection has gone dead, I sit there with the dial tone buzzing in my ear. I replace the receiver and look at Gran, but she already knows.

"When do you need to go?"

"She said ten days."

Gran looks surprised. "Why such a long wait?"

"The doctor said something about Jamie needing chemotherapy before they can perform the operation."

"Are you sure about this?" Gran asks, the lines on her forehead deepening with concern.

I think about the question, then try to explain. "I think that's why I'm here, Gran. I mean, not here on earth or anything. But somehow — it's why Mom and I came to the farm this summer. One of the reasons, anyway. As soon as Mac told me about the test, I had a feeling my bone marrow would match. Even when I met Jamie — before I knew who he was — I felt, I don't know, connected somehow. Does that sound weird?"

Gran's eyes are full but she smiles the first smile I've seen in a week. She looks young again. "Not a bit." Then her face gets serious. "You have to tell your mother."

"Couldn't you?" I ask, suddenly a coward.

"It's something you need to do, dear. You need to tell her how you feel." She says this so strongly that it feels as if she isn't just talking about me and my mother.

I go upstairs and stand outside my mom's door for a very long time. I hear her moving around inside. I hope this is a good sign.

I knock tentatively. Her voice sounds strong as she calls, "Come in," and I feel a stab of hope.

But the first thing I see when I open the door is her suitcase on the bed, half filled with neatly folded clothing.

"What are you doing?" I ask stupidly.

"I need to get back to work, Claire. I'm just not getting enough done around here. We'll leave first thing in the morning."

She says this as calmly as if she's announced the weather forecast.

"The hospital called," I say. "I'm a match for Jamie. Surgery is in ten days. I can't leave."

Mom doesn't even look at me. "If that's your choice, I can't stop you. Your father can sign the permission forms. I will have no part in this."

"You can't be serious." I am stunned.

"We all make our choices, Claire. I've said I won't stop you."

"But you're leaving me!"

Mom pales at this. "No. But I am leaving. I want you to come with me." Her eyes plead, and for a second I'm tempted to rush over and hug her and agree to anything that will keep us together.

We look at each other for a long while, each willing the other to cross over. Then she turns away and I leave the room quietly.

I sit down heavily on the edge of my bed. I hate her.

"I hate you," I say out loud, but I know it's not true. I only wish I did.

18

The next morning, when I go downstairs for breakfast, Gran is alone in the kitchen. She offers to make breakfast, but I'm not hungry.

"She wants me to go home with her, Gran."

She nods, but doesn't say anything.

"How can I leave Jamie? I can't."

"Then you've made your choice, dear."

"But what if she never forgives me?"

"She will."

"You don't know that. Look at what happened between her and Gramps!"

Gran flinches, as though I've struck her.

"I'm sorry," I say quickly.

"Don't be. You're right to wonder about that. Lord knows I've gone over it myself — again and again. I've often wondered if things would have been different if I'd — as you said the other day — banged their heads together and said, "Listen to each other.'"

"Why didn't you?"

Gran sighs. "That's not the way it was between your grandfather and me."

"How was it then?"

"I was raised to believe that you supported your husband, no matter what. He was the head of the household — the man of the house — you see. I suppose that sounds very old-fashioned to you."

"Kind of," I admit. "Then again, we never really had a man around the house ..."

"You know, after Abe died, I wandered around this place lost — in my own home. For the first month, I got up, made breakfast — bacon and eggs, Abe's favorite — and brewed a pot of coffee like I'd done for the last forty-seven years. Then one day it occurred to me ... I don't like bacon and I hate coffee!"

Gran says this so forcefully that it almost makes me laugh.

"I mean, I really hate coffee. I hate the way it smells. I hate the way it makes me feel. I just ..."

"Hate it?"

Gran smiles a little. "Isn't that silly? And whoever told me I couldn't steep a pot of tea in the morning? No one!"

"Um, what does this have to do with —"

Gran takes my hand and strokes it absently. "I loved your grandfather very much, Clarissa. And he loved me. We had many, many lovely moments — long walks in the country, hours of Scrabble in the evening. And at night he would take me in his arms and hold me — so tight." A tear trickles down her cheek.

I reach over and wipe it away with my hand.

"I knew how much he loved me and how much he loved Janey, and I thought it would see us through ..."

"But it didn't."

"No, it didn't. He was so determined to protect her from the big evil world — keep her safe in his small world. And she was just as determined to break free. It became a battle of wills and finally, she had to leave."

"And he never forgave her for that?"

Gran looks almost surprised. "Well, that's another matter entirely," she says crisply. "In order for your grandfather to forgive your mother, he would have had to let go of all the things he'd grown to trust. His sense of propriety — of right and wrong. And this, dear Clarissa, he could not do. He didn't possess enough ... faith ... to let go of these things."

I'm struggling to understand, but there's nothing solid enough to grab on to. "So he still loved her?" I repeat this to make it real to me.

"He loved you both."

"But he kept it all inside. It's such a ... waste."

"There were things he was never able to say, but he found ways to ... express them."

I look at her curiously.

"His hands, Clarissa," she says finally.

"His hands?"

But Gran just shakes her head. "Not now, dear. Another time."

~ ~ ~

When Mom's car is packed Gran and I go outside to say good-bye.

Gran hugs Mom and promises to take me to the airport when it's time. Mom will send the ticket.

To me, Mom says, "You'll keep practicing the piano."

I nod, dumbly, wondering how she can think of something so unimportant. Doesn't she realize nothing will ever be the same again?

Gran and I watch as her car drives out of the yard. When only the dust remains, we go back into the house. We can't say it out loud, but it's as though a dark cloud has lifted.

Maybe it's guilt, but I go to the music room and sit down at the piano. I've been avoiding it because it feels like my mother's dream, not mine. I skim through my music, but the notes run together in a meaningless rattle of noise. Instead, I look through the sheets in the bench and pull out a sonata by Beethoven. It's difficult.

It takes some time, but eventually I coax a tune from the keyboard, staring intently at the notes. When I realize Gran is standing in the doorway, I stop playing, embarrassed.

"Beethoven must be twirling in his grave," I say apologetically.

"Oh no," Gran reassures me, then adds, "a little concerned, perhaps." We both laugh.

"That was your grandfather's favorite," she says, sitting down beside me.

"Really? I thought he liked only sacred music?"

Gran shakes her head. "Oh no. He loved the hymns — found them comforting. But it was the more complicated pieces that he really enjoyed, especially the way your mother played them."

"How did she play them?" I ask.

Gran thinks about this. "The way the composers hoped they would be played, I suspect. It was a sad day for your grandfather when she gave up her music."

"Did he ever tell her? That he missed the music?"

Gran shakes her head. "There wasn't time. By then there were other considerations."

Other considerations. Me. I was the other thing that had to be considered.

The wind is rustling through the trees outside. From where I'm sitting, I can see the tops of the tomato vines gently swaying. I imagine Gramps out there, quietly standing — leaning against his hoe. I continue playing, determined to conquer the Beethoven.

I spend most of the week at the hospital with Mac and Jamie. Jack drives me when he can. Sometimes I catch a ride with Gran or people she knows from church.

The chemo is destroying the cancer cells and Jamie's bone marrow. The doctors call this "conditioning." Such an upbeat name — like all the sunshiny colors on the walls. They're killing him, slowly, and it's up to my cells to rescue him. That's the medical term — cells rescuing cells. It scares me. What if my cells fail? Does that mean I've failed?

When I walk into the hospital room, Mac's reading to Jamie. *Sir Gawain and the Green Knight*. Jamie doesn't seem to be listening, but when Mac stops to greet me, Jamie moans and opens his eyes. There's a flicker of recognition but no smile. To smile would take more energy than he can spare.

"Hey, Sir Lancelot," I say quietly.

There's no answer. Mac glances up at me, his eyes dark and tired-looking. "He's having a rough day."

I pull up the chair on the other side of his bed. "Hey, Jamie, I was thinking — maybe when you're finished getting better you could come with your dad to visit me in Toronto?"

There's no answer from the bed.

"That's a great plan," Mac says, a little too enthusiastically.

Jamie groans softly and I can see a spasm of pain travel across his face. Mac lifts a pan to Jamie's mouth in case the little boy needs to vomit, but the spasm passes and his small frame relaxes. Mac slowly, mechanically, lowers the pan.

I feel so useless and I'm tempted to leave — the room, the building, the sickness and the stupid animals on the walls.

"What would we do?" Jamie asks in a voice so soft I can barely make out the words.

I'm not sure if this is the mental confusion Dr. Fielding warned us about. Mac shrugs.

"In Toronto," Jamie adds.

"Oh," I say. "Well, first of all you'd come to our apartment and clean my room. It's always a huge mess. And then, well, you could take out the garbage and wash the floors, water the plants ... oh, and clean the windows. We're eleven floors up."

A barely perceptible smile crosses Jamie's lips. "No," he mutters.

"Why not?" I say. "I could hang you over the ledge by your toes and you could wash the windows with a squeegee!"

He smiles again but then another wave of nausea comes and he throws up weakly into the pan. When he's done, Mac wipes his chin. I feel the pressure inside my head gather like a thunderstorm.

"What next?" Jamie asks softly.

I choke back my tears. "Well, then I take you to see Julia. She's my best friend. She'll go nuts over you. She loves little kids — got an A+ on her baby-sitting exam. She'll call you silly names like 'Sugar Lump' and probably kiss you on the nose."

Jamie wrinkles his tiny nose at this. "You could," he says.

I lean over, and as I come close to his small face, a sour smell hits me. I move past it and touch the narrow, hard ridge of his nose with my lips.

When I sit back into my chair, he says, "You can have my sword if you want."

In the corner of the room, leaning against the paw of a congenial-looking squirrel, is his dragon-slaying sword.

"You're going to need it, kiddo. You have to fight Alonzo," I say, my voice breaking.

Jamie closes his eyes. I can see the strength it takes to push them shut. A tear forms in the corner of each eye as he shakes his head slowly, so slowly. "Uh-uh," he says. "I can't anymore."

Mac's face dissolves. I can't bear to look at him.

"You know what?" I'm hoping that all of Jamie's seven-year-old instincts haven't been swallowed by the chemo.

"What?" he responds faintly.

"I think that, compared to you, Sir Lancelot is a great big weenie."

To my surprise, Jamie giggles, a frail echo of his real laugh, but still a laugh.

"He is not," he asserts, his voice stronger now.

"Well, compared to most people he's pretty terrific. But compared to you, well," I lift my hands in defeat, "there is no comparison. You're the bravest person I've ever met."

Jamie lifts his eyes to me and I can see deep inside the pain. His fear is so open that I can barely hold back my tears.

"You are, you know. No matter what, you're the bravest person I know."

I reach over and take his hand. His skin is warm and dry, but he squeezes my fingers and I can feel the life inside — tired and worn.

I squeeze back and then his hand relaxes. His breathing is soft and regular. I let out a breath, unaware that I've been holding it in, and I feel the exhaustion move over me — a slow, rocking wave.

"He's sleeping," Mac says, gesturing for us to leave the room.

Once we're outside the door, Mac pulls me toward him, giving me a tentative hug. I cling to him.

"Thank you," he whispers into my hair.

I pull away to look into his eyes. They're the same color as Jamie's — a deep blue. The same color as mine.

"But I don't know if it will work. Maybe my cells won't take ..."

"No," Mac says firmly. "Thank you for making him laugh."

I know making Jamie laugh is not enough. It's not nearly enough.

❧   ❧   ❧

The second week is worse. I feel like I'm hanging on to a thin wire by my fingertips. I take up running when I'm not at the hospital but it doesn't help.

And then one day, I meet a nurse on my way back from the cafeteria. She has tears in her eyes and almost runs me down.

"Are you all right?" I ask, steadying her.

"Not really," she admits, rummaging through her pocket for a tissue.

I give her one of mine.

"Jennifer. She didn't make it …" she says, wiping her nose. "We get so attached to them. I'm sorry." And then she's gone.

I look into the room she's just left. Jamie's friend, Jennifer. Her family is standing around her bed, grieving. I am an intruder, and back away.

For the first time, I realize that Jamie could die. A sharp pain fills the side of my head and I feel the tears burn behind my eyes. I run down the hall and through the building until I'm outside, sucking in the misty, rain-washed air like a drowning person.

Jack finds me twenty minutes later.

"There you are. I thought we were supposed to meet at Jamie's room. Are you okay?"

I nod woodenly. "Is he okay?"

"He was sleeping." Jack's eyes are pushing me to talk, but I look away."Can we go somewhere? Not home."

So Jack drives me to the ocean. Spanish Banks, he says it's called. There aren't many people. Mothers lean against bleached logs with their books, huddled in blankets while their kids dance about carrying buckets, screaming when they find an empty crab shell or a seashell.

"I'm sorry it's not sunny," Jack says. "It's even more beautiful then."

There's a fine rain, more of a mist. It's the first rain since the day of the church potluck.

"It's pretty," I say, knowing Jack wants me to find it beautiful.

"You should see it on a nice day," he says eagerly. "We'll have to come back another time." I find myself resenting his efforts to cheer me up.

"Have you ever noticed how many different shades of gray there are?" I ask, watching the dappled water lap softly against the shore. I'd expected crashing waves breaking over the beach. The calm indifference of these waves disappoints me.

"When I was a kid, I loved the expression, 'slate gray.' I don't know why. I used to describe everything ... the water of Lake Ontario, the sky during a storm, how I was feeling ..." My voice drifts away, and I can see Jack straining to hear my words before they're carried by the wind out to the charcoal sea.

The hazy outline of the North Shore mountains is barely visible now, and I wonder if this is how my mother feels when she's having one of her migraines. I can see how she could let herself dissolve into darkness. It would almost be a relief to let it fold over me, to lose myself in the hopelessness of it.

"There's so much gray," I whisper, shivering for the first time in weeks.

Jack points to a shimmering sliver of yellow light drawn by the faded sun through the clouds. "Over there," he says. "That's not gray."

I nod. But it's so thin and weak.

"I can't go back," I whisper.

"Home?" Jack asks, bending closer to me to hear.

"No," I wrap my arms around my knees. "To see Jamie."

"You don't want to do the transplant?" He's trying to keep the shock out of his voice.

"No, no," I say, rubbing my legs to warm them. "I'll do the transplant. I just can't see him again. I can't watch him ..."

We get so attached to them. The nurse's words clang in my head.

The wind pushes against me, and the drizzle turns into a sharp, cold rain. "Can you take me home now, Jack?"

19

I have four days before the procedure. Time to kill. Wanting to kill time when it's so precious to Mac and Jamie is horrible. Still, that's what I need to do. I try to keep busy, but everything around the farm reminds me of death. Some of the leaves are turning, and harvesting has begun, trees have given up their fruit, the evening air is brisk. All endings.

Gran makes conversation as I help her with the chores, but she doesn't pry. Jack keeps calling. I tell Gran I don't want to talk to him. I avoid him when he comes to work by staying in my room. One day I notice him standing in the middle of the yard. I know he can't see me but he's looking up at my window, just standing there ... waiting. Finally he walks away heavily.

Two days before I'm due to check into the hospital, Mac calls.

"I can't talk to him, Gran," I plead as she holds out the receiver.

"Yes you can," she says in a tone I've never heard before. It's kind but determined. I take the telephone reluctantly.

"Clarissa?" Mac says hesitantly. "Is that you?"

"Hi, Mac." I try to sound normal.

"How've you been? Are you all right?"

"Everything is fine. How's Jamie?" I hate the casual note in my voice. I hate how believable I sound.

"It's, um, he's holding on. Clarissa, tell me, is something wrong?"

"Claire. It's funny — everybody here thinks of me as Clarissa. But I've never actually been called that."

There's a long pause at the other end of the line.

"Okay. Claire." Mac's voice has gone neutral and stiff. "Jamie has been asking about you."

"Tell him that, um. Tell him I ..." A lump forms in my throat, so I cough. "I said hi. I'll be there, Mac," I add quickly. "I have to go. Bye."

I hand the receiver to Gran and run out of the house. I can't look at her.

I run and I run and I run. Up the driveway, across the road to a field where I've never been before, a field of stubble. I don't know where I'm going, but eventually I turn back, past the birdhouse tree, pulled toward the place where I met Jamie.

I collapse on the boulder beside the brook, exhausted now. I wait for something terrible to happen. I deserve it. I've abandoned a little boy who needs me. But nothing happens and I start to cry. I cry for Jamie. And Mac. Then for my mother and my grandfather and, eventually, I cry for myself until it turns into a prayer. When I'm finished, I expect the fear to come back, but it doesn't. It's as though there's nothing left for it to grab hold of anymore — it's been released into something bigger and more powerful.

I watch the water move in its slow, steady current, and the stillness fills me. The crying was horrible, but the numbness I've felt all week — the dull, empty ache — was far worse.

I stand up and throw rocks into the water. The ripples stretch into wider and larger circles until the center is smooth again and peaceful. And that's how I feel, deep in the center. I can feel again.

All of a sudden a massive head appears over the top of the hill across the small stream. It's the bull — Jamie's dragon. I consider running away, but I yell at the huge beast instead. "Go away! Get out of here!"

The animal crooks his huge head like he's saying "Who's bigger? You or me?"

I take a step and feel the water rush into my sneakered foot. "You're nothing but a big bully. Get out of here!" I scream. The bull turns and, with a flick of his long tail, he is gone.

I stand there for the longest time, in case the bull comes back. Stupid bull if he does, because

I'm feeling stronger every minute. I'd welcome a chance to bellow and rant some more.

"That's telling him," a voice calls out.

Jack is standing at the edge of the woods.

"How long have you been there?" I demand, embarrassed.

"Long enough," he says, craning his neck over the meadow. "Look, he's heading for the hills, his tail between his legs. No, wait, he's calling out to the cows," Jack puts his hand to his ear. "Run for your lives, there's a maniac loose. Save yourselves ..."

I laugh. I had no idea I'd missed him so much.

"I'm glad you're here," I say, surprising myself, and evidently Jack as well, because he looks doubtful.

"Really? The way you've been avoiding me, I thought ... I ... What did I do?" he asks in a small voice. He reaches out to pull me up the mossy incline. His skin is warm and moist.

As soon as I'm beside him, he sits down on a log. "So?"

"I just needed to be by myself for a while. I can't really explain it. It was Jamie and Mac and the ... horror of it ..." I flail my arms around a bit, hoping that words will come to me.

"So what am I? Some fly that you just brush away? Some annoying little insect?"

The image of Jack flying around my face makes me smile, but I can see he's serious.

"I've never actually thought of you as a fly," I admit.

"You know, you have some very irritating qualities."

I gulp at this, but I know I have it coming. "Such as?"

"Well, one minute I think you like me and the next minute — nothing."

"I do like you."

"I'm not so sure I like you," he says gruffly. "I mean, let's review the situation. There's all that stuff in the beginning. The whole water trough thing and the phony boyfriend and then, BANG, you need me to cart you around, so I think, yeah, we're friends. And then the kiss. That was nice. I figure I can cope with this. But then you do a complete one-eighty and get all withdrawn and I think it makes sense because your brother's so sick. So I try to be Mr. Helpful but *then* you won't talk to me and ... it's just all very irritating. That's it. I find you very irritating and disagreeable. But I can't stop thinking about you, which really, really, has been getting on my nerves. And I'm, like, walking around with a nauseous feeling in the pit of my gut and I ask myself, 'What girl is worth this?'"

He hops down to the bank below and paces.

"I do know other girls, I hope you realize. Really great girls. Girls who would actually like to be with me. Hordes of them. But every time I pick up the phone to call one of them, I see this image of your face. Not even your face. It's like this whole ghost-like eerie specter thing that floats around me. And I'm really tired of it. That's it. That's why I'm here. To tell you that I'm tired of the whole thing and to wish you good luck and, yeah. So, good luck."

He looks at me then, but makes no move to leave.

"Wow," I say. I leap down to the bank and stand opposite him. "But you thought it was a nice kiss?"

He finally smiles. A slow smile at first, tugging at the corner of his lip, then it becomes this incredibly warm grin. "You're certifiable."

I hold my hand out and count off my fingers. "Irritating, disagreeable, nauseating, what was the other one? Oh yes, eerie and now certifiable? You like me, I think."

He moves closer and I know he's going to kiss me. Everything goes slow motion, just like in a bad romance novel. Normally I'm way above this corny stuff. Honestly.

His head turns sideways a little and I can feel his warmth as he bends down and his lips touch mine. But then, suddenly, it's not bad romance-novel material: I'm there, totally and completely. And it's not perfect — our noses sort of bang and my front tooth clunks into his, but then it is. Perfect.

When we come apart I'm surprised to see everything around us looks the same. Same trees, same water. The same insolent crows caw-cawing from the trees.

Jack says nothing. I move back a step and feel the spell melt away.

"I'm glad you came here," I say again. "I'm sorry if I hurt your feelings. I —"

"You've had a lot on your mind."

"I know, but that wasn't really why I backed off. I was just feeling so terrible about what was going on with Jamie, but I didn't know how to say it, you know? My mom and me, we don't talk about our feelings so much. I thought it was just my mother, but I guess I'm more like her than I realized. I didn't know how lonely it would be to handle everything by myself. Or how hard," I say awkwardly.

Jack waits patiently.

"I'm so scared he's going to die." I finally blurt the words out, and my eyes fill up with tears. "And there's nothing I can do about it. The operation might work but it might not and I ..."

"What?" Jack asks.

I look past him over to the brook, the same even rush of water as before.

"The operation might not work ... and?" he prompts.

"All I can do is ... be with him. That's all." I look up at Jack through my tears. "Even if he dies."

Jack holds me for a long time, stroking my hair, until the tears stop. When he lets go, I can still feel the touch of his hand on my hair.

"I wish I was one of those guys who carries a handkerchief, but let's face it, those guys are usually —"

"Nerds," I finish, and we both laugh.

20

Gran and I have an early dinner, and then she drives me to the hospital to see Jamie.

We travel most of the way in silence, but at the outskirts of Vancouver, Gran asks, "What made you change your mind?"

"I couldn't let Alonzo win." The countryside rushes past the window in a purple blur.

Gran's quiet for a while and then says, "I left my code book at home, dear."

I stretch my arm along the back of the seat so my fingers touch her shoulder.

"That's the name Jamie gave his imaginary dragon. I think it has something to do with fear, Gran."

"Mm-hm," she murmurs.

When we reach the hospital she asks, "Do you want me to come with you?"

I shake my head. "I think I need to talk to them alone. Is that okay?"

"That's fine. I'll go do a few errands. I'll be back in a couple of hours, all right?"

I nod and watch her drive away.

On Jamie's floor, I say hello to the nurse at the nursing station. Lights are dimmed, the talk hushed. I've never been here this late before. She glances at her watch. "Only thirty minutes left, love, but don't worry if you want to stay a little longer."

I smile my thanks. "How's he doing?"

"Go see for yourself."

Outside Jamie's door, I peek through the glass before pushing the door open. The television is on. I can tell by the blue light that throws moving shadows across their faces. Mac is sitting beside Jamie on the bed, his arm around him. It looks like Jamie is asleep. I walk in quietly.

At first I just stand there, not sure if Mac even wants me to stay because he has an expression on his face I can't read. I sit down on a chair in the corner. Mac gets up from the bed carefully and turns off the television. Then he flicks on a small lamp beside Jamie's bed. The little boy stirs but doesn't wake up.

"You're here," Mac finally says.

"I'm sorry," I whisper past the lump in my throat.

"You have nothing to be sorry about." He pulls a chair beside mine and sits down.

"But I ran away." I don't want to be let off the

hook so easily. "I couldn't handle it."

"We all run away at some point. But you came back. That's the important thing, Clarissa. I mean, Claire?" he looks at me questioningly, and I shift in my seat uncomfortably, remembering our telephone conversation.

"Clarissa, Claire. It doesn't matter."

"You've been thrown into a tough situation, but you don't have to be Supergirl, you know? Is there still Supergirl? I've lost track of my cartoons."

I smile through my blurry vision. "I don't know. But I did want to save the day, I guess." I look down at my feet, tapping on the floor.

"You're not responsible for what happens," Mac says urgently, taking my hand. "Just the fact that you've been here for Jamie and me means everything. You must believe that."

I nod, not quite able to speak.

"And if being here is too difficult ..."

I shake my head vigorously and clear my throat. "No, it's not. I want to ... share it. That's what I found out. I wanted to run away but I couldn't, even when I did. I mean, I could run away from you and Jamie, but not from myself, and part of me is part of you two now. Boy, I'm blowing this. It was a lot clearer when I was yelling at Alonzo."

Mac chuckles. "Well, one thing's certain, you and Jamie are related!"

"Exactly! That's it. I'm related … and I want to be. Good times, bad times … awful times even, no matter what."

"You give me hope," Mac finally says.

"I do?" My heart is full.

"You have such courage. And I'm very sorry I haven't been part of your life."

I want to believe him, so much. "But, Mac … okay — you wrote letters and Mom didn't let me see them, but couldn't you have called — even once?" My voice cracks.

He chokes up, too. "I wanted to, many times. But I knew how your mother felt about me. No, that's not fair. I can't put this on her. I didn't know how to be a father until Jamie came along. And by the time I had enough confidence, he was sick, and it's all been a blur since then." He leans forward in his chair, elbows on his knees. "You know how Jamie's always pretending he's Sir Lancelot?"

I nod.

"I used to do that, too, when I was his age. But I'm no white knight, Clarissa. I'm just a guy who's trying to figure out stuff as I go along, and barely keeping up. But one thing I know for sure is that I've missed out by not knowing you."

"I don't need a white knight, just a father," I say quietly.

He smiles, and the skin crinkles around his eyes. Then he reaches for me across the arms of the chair and hugs me for a long time.

"Hey, Lady Guinevere," a sleepy voice calls out.

I sit beside Jamie on the bed. His cheek feels warm but not feverish. His eyes are still heavy with sleep, but they're clear of pain.

"Where did you go?" he asks.

"I had to fight Alonzo."

"Did you kill him?"

I wish I could say yes. "Nah, but I think I frightened him away."

"Good. He's not so bad, you know. He just likes to scare people. He's just a big old dragon." Jamie's voice slows and he blinks groggily, but there's a slight smile playing on the corner of his lips. "I'm glad you're here ..." And he sleeps again.

I pull the cover up until it brushes his chin and tuck it around his thin shoulders.

It's late by the time Gran and I are ready to head home. Mac is going to spend the night with Jamie. Dr. Fielding comes by before we leave to ask me to check in early tomorrow for a couple of blood tests before the procedure the following day. I'm excited to be closer to the day of the transplant, but I no longer have the need to kill time.

The night is bright with stars, and a full moon hangs low when we turn into the farmyard. I don't notice the car in the driveway until I hear a door slam shut and see my mother emerging from the shadows.

We both stand still, but only for a moment. Then, whatever it is that is holding us back, breaks free. We hug for a long time without speaking. Her hands caress my hair and I hold her — thinner than I remember — close. I can feel her heart beating.

"Great timing," I whisper.

"Smart ass," she says into my hair.

Checking into the hospital the next morning is an annoying waste of time. But my mother comes through and handles the medical information and room arrangements with total efficiency.

"Are you ready for this?" she asks once we're in the room.

"So ready," I answer.

I sit down on the end of my bed. "You came back."

She sits beside the bed. "I made it to the Ontario border."

"And you turned around?"

"I went south for a while but then I hit another border ... so I went north ..."

"Sounds like quite a trip."

"Oh, I saw a fair bit of this great land," she says, and we laugh a little. "But none of the other directions felt like home. I thought I could go back to Toronto and my old life, but without you there ..." The sentence dangles, but I can wait.

Mom looks out the window.

"You know, this was the first time I'd been alone — in my entire life? I lived with my parents for the first eighteen years and for the next fifteen, I've had you. But for the last while, it's just been me. I guess I had to find myself."

"And you did?"

"Yup. In Moose Jaw."

I'd thought the question was a little more philosophical. She laughs at the expression on my face.

"Seriously, Claire. I found myself in Moose Jaw. A great movie title, huh?"

I smile feebly. It's not what she's saying that's bewildering me, it's the light in her eyes.

"I was on my way back to Smallwood, but I still didn't know why. I was angry with you for not obeying me. I couldn't accept that you chose to stay here. And then, in the middle of Moose Jaw, right in front of the Dairy Queen, I think it was, I stopped the car ..."

"And went for a Buster Bar?"

She laughs at this and there are tears shining in her eyes, but the light is even brighter.

"No," she admits. "I saw a little boy — he was about to cross the street and his mother was calling for him to wait for her. I could hear the panic in her voice, so I stopped the car. He crossed anyway and when she caught up to him, she hugged him, then scolded him. She was just trying to protect him ... That made me realize that I'm still afraid to let you cross the street alone."

"I'm getting pretty good at it though, Mom."

"Yes, I can see that." Her eyes meet mine. "How did such a coward manage to raise such a courageous daughter?"

My eyes fill with tears. "You're not a coward."

"Oh, I am, Claire. I've been running away from my past for too long. But you, you get plunked in the middle of it — and do you run? No, you just take it all on."

"I don't understand."

"Why didn't my father love me enough to accept me the way I was? Why didn't my mother do more? Why wasn't Mac there for me when I needed him? I've clung to all that injustice, but you just swept through it like a tornado. On that street in Moose Jaw, I realized that I had become my father. Angry at the world, clinging to a narrow notion of right and wrong … unable to forgive and move on."

"So what did you do?"

"Well, I surprised myself. I prayed. For forgiveness. Right there on the bald prairie. Sort of appropriate, I thought, feeling as empty as I was."

Now I'm truly amazed. My mother, who I've always seen as straight and narrow as one thin line, has poetry in her. I can see the girl Mac fell in love with. She's smiling now and I see the light inside her. It's pink and orange and purple.

"You're not a coward," I insist again, my voice stronger now. "And I understand about running away. More than you know. But the important thing is that you came back," I say Mac's words to me, experiencing their truth from the other side.

"It's not too late?" she asks uncertainly.

"It's not too late," I answer and lay my head against her shoulder.

21

Later that night I start to feel nervous. Mom looks anxious as well, especially when Dr. Fielding outlines the risks, low as they are. Mom asks a million questions, and I teeter between embarrassment and relief that she cares so much. Over the last few weeks, as I've watched Jamie fight, I've come to understand fear.

"I think this is the most important thing I've ever done, Mom," I tell her after the doctor has left. "It'll be fine."

She tries to smile. "That's how I felt when I was in the hospital."

"When you had me?" I ask.

"Of course," she says, messing up my hair.

"Did you ever wonder if ... I was the right thing?" I try to sound casual.

She seems surprised by the question. "Of course not."

"But you gave up so much," I say, my voice trembling now, betraying me. I can't look at her.

She turns my head gently to face her. I take one of those big shaky breaths to avoid crying.

"I've made a lot of mistakes in my life, Claire. But you were never one of them."

I desperately want to believe this, but the words in her diary haunt me. I can't help thinking this isn't the complete truth.

"But you wanted to be a concert pianist and travel the world ... and be with Mac," I say this quietly. "I changed all that."

"Listen to me," she says in her familiar stern voice. "Getting pregnant was the result of an impetuous moment and, yes, it was a mistake. Being angry at my father all those years and refusing to have it out with him was a mistake. Blaming everybody else for my unhappiness was another." She rolls her eyes. "Such a long list. But my worst mistake was trying to shelter you from all my other ones. I thought that's what parents were supposed to do — that's what my father tried to do. I realize it now. He wanted to protect me from all of the ugliness in the world."

"But if getting pregnant was a mistake ..."

Mom puts her hands on my shoulders. "Getting pregnant, Claire, was the *result* of a mistake — that brief moment in time when Mac and I decided we could play with the laws of biology. That was our mistake. But *you* were never the mistake. You were the ... the blessing that came out of it." Her eyes fill with tears. "I haven't used that word since ... forever. But that's what you've been to me. Maybe if you hadn't come along I'd be playing piano somewhere — Germany or Paris — but I wouldn't be a happier person. I've never been a very happy person — I've always strained for something more. But when I come home at the end of the day and you're there with your great smile — and your snotty attitude — my world brightens. I'm going to shake you until you believe that."

"No, no. It's okay. I believe you," I put my hands on hers. "I didn't realize that I was quite so great, but now that you mention it, it makes total sense."

She laughs. "Well, that's good. Don't you ever forget it."

It's easy to promise.

~ ~ ~

We're playing gin rummy when Mac comes in. I'm way ahead. Mom's grimacing at her cards as though this will improve her hand. When she sees Mac, she holds the cards tightly against her.

For a few seconds they just stare at each other. Suddenly I don't feel exactly in the room. It's like watching a scene in a play.

"Your mother told me you'd come back. I thought you would," he says to her.

"How could you think that, Mac? I've been awful." She doesn't say this in a pitying way. It's matter-of-fact and dignified.

Mac steps closer and Mom lays down the cards on the bedspread. "I've done my share of awful things, too, Janey."

I watch them embrace, whispering apologies. It's better than all my fantasies combined.

Eventually they remember I'm in the room.

"Jamie's finally asleep," Mac says to me. "How are you doing?"

"I'm good."

"Yes you are," he says, kissing my forehead. "Our daughter is quite something."

I look at Mom, wondering how she'll react to the "our daughter." But she just nods in agreement.

"Can you spare your mother for a bit?" Mac asks.

"Sure. I'm kinda tired," I lie.

"Do you need anything?" she asks.

"Nothing," I answer truthfully.

"Okay, I'll see you first thing in the morning. I love you," she whispers as she kisses me.

"Me too."

"How about a slice of cheesecake?" Mac asks Mom. "It's not as good as the stuff we used to steal from your mother's fridge, but it's not half bad."

My mother actually giggles.

"Have fun," I call out, and they both turn at the same time. "Don't stay out too late."

"Pretty feisty, isn't she?" I hear my mother say as they leave the room.

"I wonder where she gets that from," he answers, and I hear that giggle again.

I flip the TV on and wonder if I can get used to hearing my mother giggle. I figure I can try. Anything seems possible now.

It's only seconds after they've left when the door creaks open again. It's Jack.

"What are you doing here?" I ask.

"I thought she'd never leave," he says, slinking into the room like a burglar. "That hospital gown is very attractive."

"I thought you said that hospital laundry makes people look gray?"

"I made that up. So, how are you doing? Are you nervous?"

"A little," I admit. "Thanks for coming."

He shrugs it off. "Enough with the gratitude already. What's on?" He points to the TV, pulling up a chair and plopping his feet on the covers.

It's something with a loud laugh track. When I fall asleep, the taped audience is still laughing.

The next morning, I don't remember where I am. I sit up, look around at the bare yellow walls, and I remember. The chair beside me is empty except for a single white rose and a note.

"You're amazing. D."

I try to think of anyone I know with the initial "D," but I can't figure it out. Then the nurse comes in to prepare me for the surgery.

In the operating room later, Dr. Fielding tells me that she'll be extracting one to two litres of marrow and blood.

"Litres?" I interrupt, picturing a jug of milk filled with my bone marrow.

"It sounds like a lot, but it's only about two percent of your bone marrow. Your body will replace it in a few weeks."

I nod, reassured and then I'm asleep.

When I come to, the world is a blur of gray lines and slow-moving shapes. At first I think I'm going to be sick, but then I just feel dizzy.

Mom's face seems a little larger than usual. I blink twice. I can see concern in her eyes.

"How's Jamie?" The words come out in slow motion.

"He's pretty weak, but it went well. I couldn't be prouder of you, honey," she says into my ear.

I drift back to sleep and I dream, a druggy, sloppy dream. The bull is pawing at the ground. He is straining against a heavy chain but it holds fast. I can see Jamie in the distance. His face is in the full sunlight, his hair long and pure gold, and he is laughing.

They discharge me from the hospital the next day. Mom and Gran arrive with an armful of flowers from Gran's garden.

"They won't let Jamie have the flowers in his room since he's in isolation," Gran says. "We'll put them in a vase in front of the window so he can see them."

I'd gone to see him yesterday but I could only look through the window. They were afraid of infection — and his recovery, *if* he recovered, the doctor said, would take a long time.

"I wish I could talk to him before I go," I say as we walk down the hallway.

"I think that can be arranged," says Mac, coming up behind me. "At least for a few minutes."

In the isolation unit, the nurse helps us all on with white gowns and masks and caps and gloves. She even makes us put little slippers over our shoes to keep the germs out of Jamie's room.

When we walk into his room, I wonder if Jamie will be alarmed by all of us ghostly creatures. But he whispers to Mac in a soft, raspy voice and Mac smiles.

"He says you look like angels."

We all laugh.

Mac puts his gloved hand on his son's head and Jamie smiles faintly. He looks small and weak, but so brave — and the glint in his eye reassures me.

Jamie says hello shyly, whispering softly to my mother, "You have nice eyes."

Mom actually blushes and squeezes his hand. "You're just as charming as your father." She looks right at Mac, and a look passes between them.

I check out Gran to see if she's noticed the look. She has. Her eyes are crinkling, but neither one of us says anything.

I move closer to Jamie. "How ya doin', Sir Lancelot?"

"They said you gave me your bone marrow? Does this mean we're blood brothers?"

"Down to the bone."

"Forever?"

"Forever," I promise.

Our time is up. As we leave, I promise to come see him again. He smiles and then he's asleep.

We strip off the filmy white garments outside the room and place them in the bin. Mac walks us down to the nurse's station, where Mom has me discharged.

"I can't thank you enough," Mac says when we're alone. "Jamie's recovery is going to take a long time ..."

"Is he going to make it?" I ask uncertainly.

"Well, Dr. Fielding says he's not out of the woods yet — there are no guarantees — but between you and me ... he *is* going to make it."

I smile and nod enthusiastically.

"And when he's strong again, I'd like to take him to see you in Toronto. Your mother has agreed, if it's what you want."

I smile over at Mom, who's haggling with the nurse about some detail.

"I'd love it," I say. "Can I ask you a question, Mac?"

"Of course."

"Did you leave a white rose in my room?"

He smiles.

"What's the 'D' for?"

He looks a little embarrassed and can't look me in the eye. "Well, signing it, 'Mac' didn't seem like enough, and 'Your Father' sounded too formal. 'Dad' was presumptuous, so I thought I'd start with the 'D' and see if I can earn the rest."

"You don't have to earn anything with me."

22

I have mixed emotions as we drive out of the city, back to Gran's. It's tough to leave when I know Jamie's still fighting, but I've done what I can. I imagine him well again — hoping that this will somehow help. I can picture taking him around Toronto and showing him off to my friends. Julia will love him — she'll find the fact that I've found my father totally irresistible.

But there's a part of me that wonders if my mother will revert to her old self once we're back. And whether I'll go back to the way I was, always looking for her approval. I don't know if people can really change, I guess. Maybe that's what is at the heart of it.

When we drive into the farmyard, I'm feeling a little tired. My hip is stiff, like I've had a hard fall on the ice.

Walking into the house, Gran turns to me and asks, "How're you doing, hon? Do you want a rest?"

"I'm okay," I say quietly.

"Well, come into the kitchen and I'll fix you something to eat."

I smile at Gran's solution to life's problems. Still, her delicious baking doesn't sound like a bad idea.

But at the doorway I stop. The room is filled with flowers, and there's a big gooey cake on the table. Jack's there, too, standing beside a big banner that reads "Happy Birthday, Clarissa."

"It's my birthday," I remember, stunned.

Mom laughs. "I can't believe you forgot! Usually she starts reminding me a month beforehand," she says to Jack.

"I ... yeah, forgot!"

Gran beams as she lights the candles.

They sing "Happy Birthday." I know I'm blushing but I don't care.

"Make a wish," Mom urges.

I look around the room at all of them and pretend to consider. I think about Jamie as I blow out the candles.

As Gran cuts the cake, Mom brings out presents. I ooh and aah at the sweater from Gran and the pants from Mom. Then Mom hands me a small package. I rip the paper off — it's a leather-bound journal.

"It locks," she observes dryly, and I know she's forgiven me for reading her diary.

I smile and give her a hug. I hug Gran as well,

but stop at Jack. My mother's newfound tolerance shouldn't be tested to the max too soon.

"There's one more present," Gran announces as we finish eating the cake. "Jack helped me with it. It's outside."

Mom looks as baffled as I'm feeling as we follow Gran. The wind is blowing lightly, bringing with it the scent of flowers.

When we reach the orchard, Jack pulls out a large wrapped box from behind the tree and hands it to me. "Happy birthday," he says.

I tear open the paper and look inside. Nestled in tissue paper is a birdhouse, painted in vivid rainbow colors. It's carved more roughly than the ones in the apple tree.

"It's beautiful," I say, looking at Gran.

Gran hangs it carefully on one of the lower branches. "Count them, Clarissa."

I start at the top of the tall tree, moving in a circle until I've finished counting. "... thirteen, fourteen, fifteen ..."

"Your grandfather made these for you. One for every year of your life. He had just started on this one before he passed away." Her voice is hushed, and I see a tear trickle down her cheek as she gazes at the tree.

"It's amazing," I finally say. I can see my mother struggling for control. I put my arms around her. "It's okay, Mom." She doesn't pull away.

Jack and Gran move back to the house. My mother cries for a long time. Slow, deep sobs at first, and then a stillness. We just stand there. She doesn't try to break away; there's no twitchiness in her. Nothing. Just stillness. That's when I know that things are going to be different.

We walk back to the house arm in arm. She goes to the music room, removes a heavy green book from the piano bench and places it on the polished music stand.

The house is filled with music. She plays slowly, lovingly. And the music is sacred.